REAL JUSTICE

WEB OF LIES

BOOK TWO

KATY LEE

Real Justice
Katy Lee

copyright © 2024 by Katy Lee, all rights reserved.

Cover design by Liz Mackey

This book is a work of fiction. The names, characters, places, and incidents are the products of the author's imagination or are used fictitiously. Any resemblance to actual events, business establishments, locales, or persons, living or dead, is entirely coincidental.

All rights reserved. No part of this publication may be reproduced, stored in a retrieval system, or transmitted in any form or by any means (electronic, mechanical, photocopying, recording, or otherwise) without the priority written permission of both the copyright owner and the publisher. The only exception is brief quotations in printed reviews.

The scanning, uploading, and distribution of this book via the internet or via any other means without the permission of the publisher is illegal and punishable by law. Please purchase only authorized electronic editions, and do not participate in or encourage electronic piracy of copyrighted materials. Your support of the author's rights is appreciated.

Quotation on Scripture Page is quoted from THE HOLY BIBLE, NEW INTERNATIONAL VERSION®, NIV® copyright © 1973,1978,1984,2011 by Biblica, Inc. ™ Used by permission. All rights reserved worldwide.

To all the bookish people. You're my kind of people.

"The path of the just is like the shining sun, that shines ever brighter unto the perfect day."
~Proverbs 4:18

CHAPTER 1

MARCUS CARTWRIGHT SWIPED at his brow as he entered his law firm on W. St. Julian Street. The Savannah summer sun, sweltering already at 9 a.m. had him wishing for another dress shirt under his suit coat. The historical building stood between Ellis Square and Johnson Square, a block from the riverfront and two blocks from where his friend's body had washed up just a few days ago. Marcus walked up to the black and gold sign behind the reception desk. A gold scale of justice balanced beneath the words *Brodsky & Cartwright, Attorneys at Law*. But now with Reginald Brodsky dead, all that was left of the firm was the Cartwright. Marcus doubted he would ever change it out of respect for his business partner and even longer-time friend.

"Gloria, Diane Brodsky will be here shortly," Marcus said, leaning over the top of the high desk with his palms on the edge. "Please ready a conference room for us. Drinks and…tissues will be needed. And text me when she arrives. I need to make a call in my office. It can't be interrupted."

Gloria's efficient nod while she handled her own multiple tasks assured him that his orders would be carried out perfectly. She had been with the firm for five years, and he hoped that wouldn't change now that he was flying solo. The truth was, Reggie handled the logistics of running the business, while Marcus's talents were utilized in keeping their highest-paying clients happy. That meant most of his time was spent uncovering the dirty deeds of their opponents, details that would close cases in his clients' favor. Any other free moment he had was soaked up by the coalition formed to combat Savannah's organized crime problem—the very call he needed to make right now in private. It was time to summon his resources.

Even if he did it begrudgingly.

Marcus closed the door to his office and sat in the leather chair behind his mahogany desk. He leaned back with his cell phone to his ear to make the call that needed to be on his private line.

"Lucius, I need a favor."

"Hello to you too, brother." His twin's condescending voice grated on Marcus's nerves. But he knew that the irritation was more out of his desperation at having to contact Lucius in the first place. Desperate times called for desperate measures.

"I need to make this quick. Reggie Brodsky is dead. He supposedly drowned in the Savannah River. I don't buy it for a second. He was looking into the Moran family."

Lucius chuckled. "Again with the Morans. Will you ever let it go? Never mind, don't answer that. Why aren't you asking your coalition? Isn't that what they're there for? What happened with your partnership with the DA's Office? I thought you all were going to crack down on racketeering and organized crime." More laughter in his brother's voice came through the line.

"We're all being watched." Marcus glanced around the room, feeling a bit paranoid about someone listening in.

"Anyone could have seen that coming." Lucius sighed. "Fine, what am I looking for?"

"Evidence that the Morans killed him. Or had him killed. I plan to bring a civil case against them. If I can't catch them in the act of their illegal dealings,

I'll make sure Reggie's wife Diane is taken care of. Reggie had been getting close to proving their part in selling guns to the gangs. He believed deals were being made at their construction sites. I think they killed him and dumped his body in the river. You need to be discreet about this."

Lucius huffed. "When have I not been?"

"I'm just saying. We look alike. This can't be tied back to me."

"My hair is still black, but it's longer than yours. I'll wear brown contacts to cover the blue. And no one will ever see me in a suit. I doubt people would confuse us never mind think we're related." Lucius's realistic words settled Marcus's paranoia. After high school, Marcus had gone to college, while Lucius went into the Navy. It changed him, physically and personally. He became secretive and lived in the shadows. After the military, Marcus wasn't sure what his older brother by three minutes did with his time. Marcus figured he was now CIA, not that Lucius would ever tell him.

Marcus glanced through the glass window to the waiting room and saw Diane Brodsky had arrived. A moment later, his phone buzzed in his hand. Gloria had texted him as asked. "I need to meet with

Reggie's wife. She just arrived. Is there anything you need from me to do this?"

"When did this happen? What did the authorities determine? I'll need details and direction."

Marcus had hoped his brother wouldn't ask. "Reggie went missing last week. His body resurfaced three days later. Deemed an accident. No sign of foul play. He had…well, he and Diane had been in a fight, and he went for a walk."

"And you jump to murder by the Morans? That makes sense." Lucius's sarcasm grated on Marcus as always.

"It does when you know they always have their hand in everything, one way or another."

"Including who their daughter dates."

Of course, his brother went there. "Christina has nothing to do with this. That was twelve years ago. They've probably married her off to some business tycoon who will join them in their crimes. I was too clean for her."

"You mean too good for her." Lucius cut quickly to the heart of the matter. "Truth is you never trusted her just because of her last name."

"I loved her."

"You used her. Don't kid yourself. Just like this

coalition partnership with the prosecutor's office. The only focus you have is to get the Morans, in any way possible, whatever the costs, and at anyone's expense."

His phone buzzed again, and he could see Diane pacing the waiting room. She looked broken. Her face seemed paler than usual, her brown ponytail was off-kilter, and her eyes were bloodshot from crying.

Was she also a means to an end? He was about to convince her to bring a wrongful death lawsuit when Reggie wasn't even in the ground yet. Maybe Lucius was right about him, and he was blinded by his mission.

Marcus shook his head, unwilling to cater to such an idea. "Kids are dying on the streets from the guns the Morans are putting in their hands. They might as well be pulling the triggers. You grew up in the same home as me. We lived in the same rough neighborhood. The Moran family was serving the gangs around us then, and they still are. You know it, and I know it."

Lucius didn't respond. Marcus wondered if he had hung up on his tirade.

Then his brother spoke, his voice barely audible. "You know, if you don't let this go, you will be next."

Marcus closed his eyes but quickly opened them

to look at the newly widowed woman in the waiting room. "I will never stop. I can't. Fear of retribution never slowed me or Reggie down before. It won't now. If anything, I can add justice for Reggie to the mission. We were in this together, and he wouldn't want me to stop now. Perhaps evidence can be found that will warrant a criminal case for his murder, no matter what the ME report says."

"Would Reggie want you to put your life on the line?"

"He would want me to take care of Diane, and this is the best way I know how."

Lucius clicked his tongue. "Fine. We do this. But once we start, there's no going back. Got it?"

"Absolutely."

"No matter what the Morans throw at us. No matter what obstacles they put in our paths. No matter who they use against us. It will end with us only."

"I'm ready."

Lucius laughed once. "You only think you are, brother. These people will not play fair, and most likely lives will be lost. You're stepping on their turf, and there's no way you will be fully ready for how they retaliate. Sleep with your eyes open. I'll be in touch."

The line went dead, and Marcus put his phone on his desk. He stood and went to the door, opening it to the closest opportunity he'd ever had in taking down the Morans. Not even the coalition came this close to touching them. Not even dating their "little princess" left a mark. Unbeknownst to Reggie, his death would be the path to victory.

"Diane, I'm so grateful for your willingness to come in today and hear what I have to say. Reggie would be so proud of you."

Diane sniffed and swiped at her eyes. She lifted her head high and said, "I'll do whatever you want me to."

Marcus smiled and waved for her to walk ahead of him. "The conference room is the second door on the right."

Ready or not, the takedown had begun. After he was done, the Moran family would be finished, come what may.

CHRIS KNEW something was off when she arrived home at her New York City apartment building, and the doorman was not at his post. Donny was a fixture as old as the green awning over the door, the same color that matched his aged uniform. She looked down the dark, empty street, first one way then the other before opening the glass door. She missed the sunrise greeting he always gave her when she returned home from working late nights at the club, but she was more concerned about his absence. It wasn't like him.

Inside, she approached the wall of tiny mailboxes and did a double take when the name tag that typically read *Chris DePalo* on the front of hers was now empty. She inserted her key and breathed a sigh of relief when it opened.

The key still worked, but there was no mail.

Her roommate Sam must have brought it up already. Making her way to the stairwell, Chris took the two flights up and headed down the carpeted hallway to the last apartment door on the right.

The door stood ajar.

Slowly, Chris placed her palm on the wood door and gave it a slight push. The first sight on the other side was her pile of mail strewn about on the floor.

"Samantha?" Her voice hitched before she cleared it. "I know you're new to New York City, but you really shouldn't leave the door open. I'm kind of fond of my things and want to keep them. And that includes you."

The sound of Chris's heels clicked across the wooden floor as she slowly entered and bypassed a few envelopes and junk mail. She decided to leave the door open behind her, as things felt off.

A scan around the apartment didn't set off any warning bells. Other than the mail, everything else seemed to be in its meticulous place. The four chairs were pushed in around the table. Her line of framed photographs from the last twelve years remained in place on top of the baby grand piano that she'd inherited with the apartment when she moved in. The latest picture of her and Sam at Central Park stood front and center. They stood on the bridge and looked more like mother and daughter than roommates. But with fifteen years between them, it wasn't surprising. Chris also saw so much of herself in the young woman, and not because they both were blonde-haired with green eyes. She saw the need to be free.

Chris continued her scan of the apartment for anything out of place or stolen. The peacock blue throw pillows on her white sofa looked untouched. Then, beyond the pristine furniture, her gaze stopped at the white chiffon curtain billowing inward with the warm morning breeze. She didn't remember leaving the window open last night, but the air conditioning had been giving them trouble lately. Perhaps Sam opened it when she returned home from her night-time adventures throughout the city.

Chris turned for the hallway that led to the bedrooms. Passing the galley kitchen, she checked to see it was empty and made her way to the closed doors at the end. She tapped softly on Sam's door, but with no answer, she opened it to find it empty except for the small twin bed and a few belongings draped over open drawers. Typically, Sam slept until noon after her nights crawling across the city pubs. But her bed hadn't been slept in at all. Did Sam not return home last night? But then who got the mail? Who opened the door…and left it open?

It wouldn't be Sam's first time being irresponsible, but this went beyond typical laziness.

A sinking concern riled Chris and made her wonder why she took in these dreamers, fresh off the bus with nothing in their purses and stars for fame in their eyes.

Maybe because I was one of them once…before reality set in.

Chris faced the other door. Her own room beckoned as did sleep. Still, she reached for her cell phone and dialed Sam's number. This behavior couldn't happen again if she wanted to continue living with her.

A phone rang instantly from somewhere behind Chris's bedroom door. As she listened to the rings through the phone and through her door, anger ramped up. The household rule was to stay out of each other's rooms.

"You have a lot of nerve after everything I've done for you." Chris rushed toward the door and flung it wide.

She inhaled sharply at the sight before her. The whole room had been tossed.

No, destroyed was more like it.

The phone continued to ring, and Chris located it beneath the disordered bed. Had Sam dropped it while she upended the room?

But why?

The two of them struggled a bit but nothing out of the ordinary. Sam felt more like a little sister to her. Their age difference came through in maturity, but Chris only meant to protect Sam from a city that could eat her alive if she wasn't careful. Sam complained sometimes but never seemed angry enough to destroy her things like this. With Sam's phone left behind, all Chris could do was wait for her to return. As tired as she was after working all night running the club, sleep would have to wait. Not that she could sleep in this room now.

Chris walked back to the living room grateful Sam had left the rest of the apartment intact. The door to the hall was still open, and Chris returned to it and closed it with a soft click.

A knife protruded from the back of the door holding a piece of paper in place.

Chris screamed at the sight and couldn't focus on the message scrawled across it. Backing away, she gripped at her throat as she tried to read the few simple, yet debilitating words left for her.

It's time to come home, Christina. Your family needs you.

Below the knife, her mailbox tag was stuck as well. But the name *Chris Depalo* was written over with the name *Christina Moran* in heavy block letters.

Her real name.

Chris stepped back and mindlessly made her way to the sofa. Dropping to the edge, she wondered when they found her. Or had they always known she was in the city? Had they only been waiting to make their move? For years, she slept with the lights on. At what point had she let her guard down?

And how had they gotten in?

She looked to the opened window and stood on shaking legs. At the ledge, she pushed the curtain aside and saw they came up the fire escape. The ladder had been pulled down, and a glance over showed a swatch of green on the ground in the alleyway.

"Donny?" Chris called and climbed out quickly. She descended the rungs of the ladder until she was by his side. Blood trickled on his temple, and he groaned when she turned him over. "Oh, thank God you're alive. Who did this, Donny? Did you see them?"

Had her father come for her himself, or had he sent her brother or one of his goons?

Donny's eyes opened, and he winced. Then he pushed up abruptly to reach for her. "Chris!"

She pushed him back down. "I'm okay, but Sam is gone. They took her. I need to know what you saw."

"There were three of them. But I only saw two at first. I saw them go down the alley, and I followed them. Then a third jumped out…that's all I remember. I've never seen them before. They wore black clothes. One was bald, the other two had brown and black hair. One had a scar."

"Under his right eye?" she asked, knowing exactly who that man was.

"Yeah, how'd you know?"

"I gave it to him." Tears filled her eyes. How foolish she had been to think her family would leave her alone forever. Her brother had found her.

"You did? You know those men?"

Chris ignored the question. "Did they say anything to you?"

Donny paused and closed his eyes again. He shook his head, then said, "Wait, yeah, the one with the scar. He said something."

"What, Donny? What did he say?"

Donny opened his eyes, and his gaze narrowed on her. "He said this was family business and to stay out of it. Are they really related to you? Those men were dangerous. I need to call the police."

"You can, but they're long gone. And they'll cover their tracks. The police have never been able to catch them before." Chris stood and helped him up.

"You said they have Sam?"

"It looks that way. I have no choice but to go after them."

"Where are you going?"

Chris swallowed hard. "Home."

CHAPTER 2

"IS THIS THE RIGHT PLACE?" The driver of Chris's rideshare car pulled up to the three-story house on Gryphon Street. As far as Chris could tell nothing had changed since she walked out the double front doors and descended the staircase to the cab that had waited for her twelve years ago. The white stucco looked pinker than the last time, but that was typical with the red bricks beneath bleeding through. Her father was behind in touching up the white paint. Not that she cared.

"Yes, this is it. Thank you for the ride."

Chris grabbed the single duffle bag she had thrown together from what she could salvage from her destroyed room back in her apartment and opened the rear door. The hot humidity hit her in the face. She'd forgotten how brutal a Georgia August could be. Stifling, really.

"Nice house," the driver said as she stepped foot on home turf.

"It comes with strings," Chris replied and shut the door without a goodbye.

Staring up at the elaborate structure, she stopped her gaze on the third-story window in the right corner. Her childhood room never looked more like a prison cell until this moment. Would Sam be in there? Would her family make it that easy for her?

Only one way to find out.

She hefted the bag up on her shoulder and ascended the stone steps without using the iron railings. At the double doors, she used her old key, surprised they hadn't changed the locks. But then it was never about keeping her out.

The center table in the foyer held the typical flower arrangement of blossoms as big as a face. The house was still and quiet, and she took the opportunity to make her way to the spiral staircase to her left, glad she wore tennis shoes with soft soles.

At the fifth step, she heard a noise from above. A lift of her head showed her father at the top. Chris halted, her hand clutching the smooth railing for dear life. The formidable Vincent Moran glared down at her. But their standoff couldn't last forever, and she couldn't let him set the stage for her time here.

"Where is Sam?" she asked with as much bravado as she could fake.

His face remained stoic. "I haven't the slightest idea of what you're talking about." He took the first step down.

Chris swallowed through a parched throat. Had she made a mistake in coming here? She had no choice.

"My roommate. The young woman you kidnapped from our apartment. Where is she?"

"I have never been to your apartment." He took two more steps. "But I'm glad to see you understand reason and have come home. Welcome back, Christina. You chose wisely."

"I'm not staying. I'm here for Sam only."

Two more steps. "There is no Sam here." He nodded to something behind her. A quick glance showed two men in suits at the bottom of the stairs.

"I should have known your goons would be waiting." She glared back up at her father, who now was three steps closer. "After what you did to my apartment. Are these the men you sent to toss my place?"

"Your place is here. It has always been here." His

hand glided down the same railing her sweating hand gripped tightly. "And no, these are not the men I sent to ask you to come home."

"*Ask?*" she couldn't have heard him correctly. "Don't you mean force?"

Her father looked out the window behind her. "As far as I could see, you came here willingly. I watched you step out of the car. You used your key, which I'm pleased you kept all these years. Somewhere deep inside, you knew this would always be your home."

"A symbol of my time in a prison." She held the key up but still couldn't let it go. Was he right in his thinking? Why couldn't she throw it away?

"I'm sorry you feel that way, my daughter." He stopped five steps from her. A glimpse of pain flickered in his gray-blue eyes, and she dropped her gaze to his black shoes. How quickly he played on her emotions. How quickly she let him. "I was actually quite happy to see you step out of that car. Your mother would have run to meet you in tears of joy. Maybe I should have, but I held back. Do you really not want to be here?"

She lifted her face to his. "No. I am only here for Sam, and then I will be gone forever. And don't call me daughter ever again. I am not part of this family."

After a moment of vacant expression that hid his emotions, he nodded once. "Your brother—I mean *Silas*, went to bring you back. He has not arrived yet. If your Sam is with him, I will find out and have her returned immediately."

"You will?" Another trick up his sleeve, she thought.

"Kidnapping is illegal. I can assure you I had nothing to do with taking your roommate. There must be a misunderstanding. I will make sure she is safe *if* she is even with Silas."

Chris realized she had no proof Sam was kidnapped. Sam might have arrived home and seen Silas and his men in the apartment. She could have dropped the mail and run back out. But why not call the police about a break-in? Or call her at the club? Sam would have no place else to run to. Unless she didn't want to lead the men to Club Creare and to Chris. Had Sam been trying to protect her?

"Until then, I do hope you will make yourself comfortable here."

"I'm not staying in this house." She looked up at the closed doors above. "But if what you say is true, I'm sure you won't mind if I look through the rooms to make sure she's not here."

He glanced at the men behind her. Then he

stepped aside and waved her on. "The house is all yours."

Chris hesitated for a moment, half expecting to be grabbed. She quickly headed past her father, bracing for anything he would try.

"The house has always been yours, Christina." He spoke so low, she paused to hear him, her eyes closing to keep from leaning into him. Even knowing the criminal acts her family committed didn't change the fact that they were only family she had ever known. No matter how many young women she invited into her life, they would never be her family.

"I'm not a Moran anymore." Her words were meant more to remind herself and not just her father.

"A hundred name changes cannot erase the blood that flows in your veins. You will always be a Moran."

Chris picked up her pace to race to the top of the stairs and through every room of the house, above and below. When she came up from the basement, she found her father sitting at the dining room table with a letter in front of him. His two guards stood behind him by the curtained window. Her steps slowed for the first time since her search for Sam began.

"As I told you, your friend is not here. But I have talked to Silas."

When he didn't go on, Chris moved closer to the table, reaching for the back of the ornate wooden chair across from him.

"Where is she? Where did he take her?" She tightened her grip on the wood. Her father took notice and sniffed.

"You two have always had it out for each other. I should have put a stop to it early on."

"But you didn't."

He smirked. "Only because Silas was always right about you. He knew you would leave us. So, I have to believe he's right again and knows what it will take for you to help us now."

And there was the catch.

Chris tilted her head, letting her long blonde hair fall off her shoulder. "Of course you want something. I didn't believe for a second you actually wanted me home." She scoffed and shook her head at his deceitfulness. "I'm not helping you with anything."

"Do you want to know where your friend is?"

"How dare you. You have put an innocent young

woman in jeopardy all because you want to control me. She's barely eighteen. She's practically a child. I won't hesitate to tell the police you were a part of her kidnapping."

He raised the palms of his hands. "I'm clean. I had nothing to do with it."

"Right. That's your excuse for every dirty deed that transpires around you. I will not join you in them. You can forget it."

"I would never ask you to put yourself in harm's way. Or to break the law. I have other people for that. All I'm asking is that you talk to an old friend and...*convince* him to leave me alone."

Chris bit back the question on her tongue. *Who is this old friend?* As soon as she asked it, she would be sucked back in with no way out. Her father pushed the envelope toward her. The name on the return address stamped in the corner became clear and saved her from asking.

"No," she said, shaking her head. "Just no."

"Mr. Cartwright seems to think I killed his partner."

Chris inhaled sharply. "Reggie's dead? You killed Reggie? How—"

"I did no such thing." Her father stood and leaned over the table. "Brodsky and Cartwright have been a thorn in my side for years. I would be stupid to kill either of them. Seeing the conviction in your eyes proves my point. My own daughter thinks I'm guilty. It won't be hard for Marcus Cartwright to find witnesses to say it in court. This case needs to go away. And you're the only person who can convince him to look elsewhere."

"Me? Have you forgotten how things ended between us? He used me to get to you. I mean nothing to the man."

Her father chuckled. "Then a chat with him should be quick. One conversation with him is all I'm asking."

"Or what?"

He shrugged, and she had her answer. She may never see Sam again.

"There had better not be one hair out of place on Samantha's head." Chris pivoted and headed for the front door. She opened it wide, yearning to breathe the thick humid air over the chokehold of Vincent Moran's death grip.

"Goodbye, daughter." Her father's voice and message carried loud and clear as she stepped outside.

Like it or not, Christina Moran was back.

MARCUS RAN along the riverfront on his typical morning jog, approaching the location where Reggie's body had been found. He had already searched the area for any clues and spent longer than necessary torturing himself with the lack of answers. Still, he turned and let his attention be pulled to where he had watched Reggie's body be zipped up in a body bag and taken away.

Marcus picked up his pace and pushed harder in his run. He had done everything he could. All the pieces were in place for the ultimate takedown. Vincent Moran had been served the litigation documents. He would have his day in court, and Marcus would be ready with ironclad witnesses. When this was all done, Moran would be broke, but hopefully, he would have enough evidence to lead to Moran's arrest in a criminal case. The dynasty would be over.

Marcus found himself smiling, his spirits lifted by a determination for justice. He turned the corner to his townhouse and saw a woman sitting on his stoop. The adjacent live oak with its hanging Spanish moss shadowed her face. But as he slowed his steps and focused, he knew Vincent Moran had counter-served his own surprise.

She stood to her full six feet and met him eye-to-eye at the landing of the stairs.

She was more beautiful than ever. Twelve years of maturity looked good on her.

"I see your father brought out the big guns." Marcus swiped at his brow. "Long time no see, Christina. What have you been up to? Your daddy kept you quite hidden. He must be scared if he's letting you out now."

"I'm not here by choice, but *I* kept myself hidden, not that it worked. I even changed my name."

"To what?"

"Never mind. Listen, I'm just as excited to see you as you are to see me, but my father can be persuasive."

"Save it. I'm not interested in anything he has to say. He's going down. Now, if you'll excuse me, I need to get ready for work." Marcus stepped up the first step.

Christina touched his forearm, halting him cold. Even in the day's rising heat, he shivered at her touch.

"I'm sorry about Reggie," she spoke low with genuine sadness in her large sea-green eyes. "I know how close you were."

He didn't respond but looked over her shoulder to a squirrel scurrying up a tree.

"How is Diane?"

He locked his gaze on her. "She'll be better after your family pays for what they did to her husband."

Christina frowned. "He says he had nothing to do with it, Marcus."

"And I'm supposed to believe a word from his mouth, or rather from the prodigal daughter's mouth."

"I haven't returned home."

"Then why are you here doing your father's bidding once again? If you really escaped as you say, then why would you vouch for him now?"

"I don't agree with my father's business practices, but you're accusing him of murder."

"Wrongful death, actually. But I do hope to have the evidence in place after the lawsuit for a murder charge. Will you come out of the woodwork for that too? I'll be sure to be more presentable next time."

She dropped her hand and smirked. Even a snide smile brought out more of her beauty. "Thank you," she said.

"For what?"

Her wide eyes which always made him catch his breath now cut him down in a different way. "For reminding me you could never be trusted. Have a nice life, Marcus." She turned toward the street corner.

"Hey, at least I got a goodbye this time," he called to her retreating back. "Sort of."

"You get what you deserve," she replied without a backward glance. "Consider yourself warned."

He huffed and headed inside as he mumbled, "Once a Moran, always a Moran."

CHAPTER 3

THE CADENCE of Chris's footsteps along the sidewalks of historic Savannah matched the rapidly beating heart in her chest. Why did Marcus Cartwright still have such an effect on her? His cavalier attitude, him acting as though they never meant anything to each other only hurt more. She had once believed she would marry him and spend the rest of her life with him. He was smart and kind. He made her feel special and seen. She didn't care that he didn't come from money, and she didn't care that her father hated him. Perhaps, she loved him more because of those things. In the end, her father had been right about Marcus. He used her to get to him, and everything their relationship stood on fell to pieces. Not one word or vow that came out of his mouth had been true. Not one "I love you" came from his heart. She had been nothing but a means to an end, and she wouldn't forget that ever again.

The phone in her back jeans pocket buzzed. Removing it, she saw it was her business partner at the club. She shot off a text that she would be gone for a few days and couldn't explain. She knew she owed her business partner an explanation for taking off without notice, but no one from her new life knew about her roots. Chris wasn't ready for her worlds to meet. How could she give explanations when she didn't know the answers herself? The idea of moving someplace else and changing her name again crossed her mind, but the fact that her family found her only proved that wasn't the answer. And how many friends could she just keep leaving behind as though they never meant anything to her? Rafe Sinclair and Melody Stiles were a huge part of her present life, but then so was Diane Brodsky from her past one.

Chris found herself two streets over from Diane's house and wondered if subconsciously she meant to go there. Unsure if Diane would even open the door, Chris continued to make her way to her old friend's house. Did she really have a right to knock on the door after leaving Georgia and everyone behind without a goodbye? At the time she believed she was protecting her friends, whether they saw it that way or not.

Chris passed numerous glass storefronts along Wells Street, slowing her steps as she approached the single detached brick home that Diane and Reggie had purchased after they married 15 years ago, two high school sweethearts completely in love. It had been run down and boarded up for years before they moved in and rehabbed it while Reggie went to college and law school. Seeing it now in all its splendor, Chris appreciated the work the couple had put into it. She stood on a street corner unable to force herself to cross over. A horse and buggy full of tourists slowly moved down the street, and she let the clopping of the horse's hooves calm her nerves.

"Are you just going to stand here spying on my home?" A voice from behind caught Chris unaware. A quick turn showed Diane behind her with two bags of groceries.

"You scared me," Chris said, clutching her chest. "I wasn't spying, honest. I...I'm not exactly sure how I ended up here. I went to see Marcus, and I was concerned about you. But I understand if you would rather I left."

Diane lightly shrugged. "There is the fact that I'm

suing your family. It's probably best if you're not here."

"I understand." Chris took a step backward.

"But I would like you to come in. I think there are things that need to be said."

"Are you sure?"

Diane pressed her lips together in a moment of indecision. "We won't talk about the case. Deal?"

Chris smiled and stepped back closer, lifting her arms to take a bag. "Deal."

They headed around the back to the rear door, passing through a fenced-in courtyard. Most of the flowers were gone from the trees, leaving lush green leaves and buzzing insects flying about. They walked up the gray stepping stones to the door, and Diane unlocked it with her free hand.

"Pardon the mess. I haven't been up to cleaning since…well, since Reggie went missing."

Chris stepped inside the kitchen and absorbed the feel of the place. A black-and-white checkered floor extended toward a formal living room with ornate, Southern furniture.

"You kept the floor," Chris remarked, toeing one of the blocks.

"Took many hours and a strained back to get them this shiny." Diane put her bag on the counter and reached for Chris's. As she emptied them, Chris continued to walk around the kitchen. She came to the table and chose the chair in the corner to sit in.

"So, what did you want to talk about?" Diane asked without turning around. She opened the refrigerator to load it up with milk and vegetables. The shelves had been empty before she did that.

"Not really sure. I suppose I should tell you where I've been for 12 years."

"That's a start." She kicked the door with her foot to close it and faced Chris expectantly.

"New York City. Silly me thought I could make it on Broadway."

"You can't sing."

Chris smiled. "That did pose a problem. So instead, I went into the restaurant business. I own a restaurant club called Club Creare now. We had some problems the past couple of years after my business partner Melody became a target of a killer."

Diane's eyes widened. "Sounds scary. I've always wanted to go to the big city, but perhaps it wouldn't be wise."

"It's fine. You'd be fine. Her stalker found her in a way that had nothing to do with the location we lived in."

"Is she safe now?"

"Absolutely." Chris smiled reassuringly. "She's married now and living in Connecticut with a great guy. I'm happy for her."

Diane's smile flitted from her face. "I hope it lasts a long time. It's unbelievable how quickly someone can be taken from you."

Chris wanted to stand up and wrap her arms around Diane but wasn't sure an embrace would be well received. She remained seated and took a few moments of quiet to consider her words.

"I'm so sorry about Reggie. He was a good man." What more could Chris say? She had been gone too long to miss him now.

"He was planning to rid the streets of your family," Diane replied matter-of-factly, her eyebrows arched in defiance.

Chris took a moment to clear her throat and hide her surprise at Diane's bluntness. "I would be the first to commend him. My father's business ethics are not my own. I run my club with the utmost respect for the law."

Diane crossed her arms and leaned against the counter. "You expect me to believe you run a club and have no ties to organized crime? Why should I trust you?"

Chris pulled her hands in front of her. Leaning

back with a sigh, she said, "All I can say is you knew I was never comfortable here. Why would I start over with a new name and a new life only to tarnish it all by cutting corners?"

"Because that's all you knew. It wasn't until you started dating Marcus that you saw anything wrong with the way your family ran their businesses. When Marcus brought you to dinner that first night we met, I nearly choked on my piece of bread." Diane laughed, throwing back her head and looking at the ceiling. "I thought he had lost his marbles by dating you."

"Gee, thanks." Chris forced a smile. "But it turned out dating me was part of his plan to get to my family, so I guess you were right about us. It wasn't real."

Diane came away from the counter and pulled up a chair. "Then I met you and spent time with you and saw you were nothing like your family."

"And yet, you believe my club is corrupt."

Diane tilted her head and slowly shook it. "No, I don't. I'm just angry, and you're sitting in front of me, the closest connection I will ever have to the Moran family. They killed my Reggie."

Chris clenched her fist before making the decision to reach for Diane's hand. "Why do you think this?"

Diane looked down to where Chris's hand covered hers but didn't push her away. "He was about to expose them for money laundering through their construction business. It was the closest crime he had ever come close to proving, and they killed him before he could."

Telling Diane that she believed her family was innocent of Reggie's murder wouldn't go over well. All Chris wanted to do was let her father know she'd kept to her end of the bargain by asking Marcus to back off. Now, she wanted to get Sam and go home to New York.

Instead, she heard herself say, "I'll look into it."

Diane covered her hand and held tight to it. "You will?" Hope filled her eyes, and Chris knew she couldn't leave just yet.

"I think I owe you that much." She stood, squeezing Diane's hand one last time before letting go. "Give me a few days, and I'll see what I can find out. But I can't promise you anything. I'm not part of this family anymore."

Diane nodded as Chris made her way to the door. "I knew I wasn't wrong about you."

Chris smiled and opened the door. As she turned

back, something shiny on the floor by the trashcan caught her attention. "Is that glass?" She took a few steps to pick it up and noticed blood was on the shard.

Diane stood and reached for it, taking it from Chris's hand. She opened the trashcan and tossed it in quickly. "It's nothing. I dropped a bottle and cut myself on it. That must've been a piece that I missed earlier."

Chris gazed into her old friend's eyes, searching for her well-being emotionally, physically, and even mentally. "If you need anything while I'm in town, please call me." She reached for a pen and a sticky note on the counter and jotted down her number, tapping it with the pen before she headed out onto the streets.

A glance back showed Diane chewing her lower lip and holding herself together.

Barely.

MARCUS STOOD WAITING for Lucius outside of the Morans' latest build site. Two sets of apartment buildings were halfway completed, but all was quiet on the construction site. Without workers around, he wondered if the build had been halted. He checked his phone for any messages and stayed in the shadow of the adjacent rundown building, also owned by the Morans. The family was involved in building new apartments as well as collecting rents as slumlords; they had their hands in everyone's pockets, one way or another.

A man walked down the street. He had a thick salt-and-pepper beard, a ponytail, and large sunglasses that covered half his face. He walked with a limp and wore dirty blue jeans and an open Hawaiian shirt over a white tank. Marcus's first thought was that he was homeless, but when the man reached him, he paused at the streetlight pole and leaned against it to light a cigarette. After the man took a few puffs, Marcus checked his phone again.

"I will never call or text you with recon," the man said.

Lucius?

Marcus felt his mouth drop in shock. "I had no idea it was you. You look nothing like me. And when did you start smoking?"

Lucius made a cutting sign at his neck with his hand and looked down the street. "Don't blow my cover," he whispered harshly.

Marcus could have kicked himself. "Right. Sorry."

"And next time, lose the suit. Are you looking to get robbed?" Lucius lowered his shades to sneer at Marcus's clothes.

"I can take care of myself. Just tell me what you have."

Lucius glanced down the street again. So far, no one had shown them any interest. A few kids were riding bikes at the far end. Another glided on a skateboard. Two old men sat on milk crates and watched the kids on this hot summer day.

"I saw the medical examiner's notes on Reggie. The notes before the report don't match the final report. A hit to the head was what really killed him, not drowning in polluted water. He was dead before he hit the water."

"Then why deem it an accident or suicide?"

"I still trying to figure that out. Someone could have convinced the ME to leave that detail out."

"By threatening him, you mean?"

Lucius let the cigarette burn as he shifted his stance and faced the unfinished buildings. He tugged on his fake beard. It held tightly to his face. Marcus wondered about the glue he used to keep it in place. Again, he wondered what his brother's line of work was since dressing incognito came naturally to him.

"Something's definitely going on at this apartment site," Lucius said. "Word on the street is the Morans received funding for building this complex for low-income tenants. But the funds aren't all going to the project. The materials are cheap, and the safety measures are being ignored. It's a risk to even walk on the site. The workers have all quit, and building has ceased."

"But I'm sure the Morans have already received the money."

Lucius nodded and scratched his bushy beard. He mumbled, "I hate these things. They make me itch." He dropped his hand and jutted his chin toward the apartments. "The half-built buildings will probably sit unfinished for eternity."

"Care to share your source?"

Lucius chuckled and shook his head. "Never. I protect my sources. Always. I care about this town too and the people in it."

Marcus looked in the other direction at the innocent boys on their bikes again. "Unlike the Morans. They couldn't care less about the people who live here. At what point do some of these kids start using the buildings for a hangout? They could get hurt, or worse." Marcus tapped the side of his fist against the building, restraining his pent-up anger. "Not that the

Morans care about the kids in these neighborhoods. They've proven they only care about themselves and their bank accounts."

"Then why send their princess?" Lucius asked.

"What? How did you know Christina came to see me?" Marcus wondered how much his bother knew.

"I wasn't talking about that. But good to know." Lucius pointed at the apartments.

Marcus dragged his attention away from the kids to follow Lucius's line of focus. A glimpse of long blonde hair pulled him from the shadows of the alley. An unmistakable tall woman who seemed to walk on air with her dancer's body entered the unfinished apartment building.

It was the so-called Moran princess that Lucius mentioned.

Christina.

A myriad of emotions hit Marcus all at once. His anger was washed away instantly when fear for Christina's safety took precedence. Panic skyrocketed his heart rate and without a second thought, he rushed into the street. Every step pounded on the pavement and then crunched in the gravel as he neared the fence of the building site at a breakneck speed.

"Christina! Stop! It's not safe!" Marcus rushed

toward the building with Lucius right behind him. In the next second, a loud crash from inside the unfinished structure shook the ground beneath his feet and stopped him in his tracks. The continuing rumble sounded like all five floors were caving in on each other. Marcus's stomach dropped just as hard. "Christina!"

CHAPTER 4

ONE SECOND CHRIS was scanning the posts and beams of the construction site as well as the state of the mess around her. Her father had never been so haphazard in any of his projects. She had walked further into the building when something dark red caught her eye.

Blood. And a lot of it. Someone had been seriously hurt here.

Or killed.

In shock at the sight of the spatter, she had backed up right into a post and heard a loud crack above her head. Running across the unfinished floors to a larger beam, she turned back and noticed the post she had hit was cracked.

Had she caused that?

Chris didn't think she had collided with it that hard. Then she heard someone calling her name, and before she could call out, the ceiling above her came crashing down and all she could do was stay close to the larger beam that held up the floors above her as every other area fell around her.

Plumes of dirt and debris filled the air around her and forced her to keep her eyes closed while she struggled to breathe. Even after the crashing ceased and the dust began to settle, Chris kept her face shielded and her eyes closed. For a moment, she wondered if she was alive, but then she felt something touch her back and knew she had survived.

Without moving from her sheltered position against the beam, she opened her eyes to darkness and realized she was barricaded by fallen debris.

Chris felt the touch on her back again, and she reached her hand behind her, fumbling until she made contact with another hand. Afraid to move one inch and cause another collapse, all she could do was hold tightly to this person.

"Are you all right?" the man asked. It was the same voice that had called out to her before the collapse.

Chris knew instantly it was Marcus, and she let the sound of his voice steady her breathing. She tried to speak, but all she could do was nod and hope he could see her.

"I think I can lift this board," another voice spoke to Marcus. "I'll hold it up while you pull her out. On three."

Chris felt Marcus's hand grip tighter as the other person counted down. As planned on three, sunlight streamed through as the crunch of wood and boards lifted and echoed around her. All at the same time, she felt another arm wrap around her waist and pull her back against Marcus's chest. Suddenly, she was falling and let out a scream. But when she landed, it was Marcus who grunted and took the brunt of the fall. He held her tight with his arms wrapped around her as he cushioned her landing.

Above her, Chris observed the collapse of the building and wondered at her survival. She gripped Marcus's hands which still had her cocooned against him. Her body trembled, and somewhere she heard whimpering.

"Shhh…you're safe." Marcus spoke into her ear from behind. "Thank God you're safe. Shhh…It's okay. I've got you."

That's when Chris realized it was her crying that she heard. "What…happened?"

"Your father happened, that's what," Marcus replied. He suddenly sounded angry.

Chris sobered instantly and tried to pull herself from his arms. "What is that supposed to mean?"

A man with a beard stepped up in front of her and offered her his arm. "This is one of your father's buildings. He's been cutting corners to save a buck. He very nearly lost his daughter today because of it."

Chris reached out and took his hand as Marcus let her go. Soon, the three of them stood on the outskirts of the rubble, staring at each other for their next move.

"I don't understand," she said. "Why would he take such a risk?"

Marcus replied, "I could ask the same question of you. What are you doing here?"

"Why can't I be here? It's my family's property." She looked back at the bearded man and squinted. "Lucius? Is that you? Why are you dressed like that?"

"Nice to see you, too," Lucius said.

"I think we can all admit this isn't a friendly gathering," Chris said, folding her arms. "What are the two of you doing here? This is my father's project."

Marcus replied, "It doesn't look like much is going on. All the workers have walked off. Care to share why?"

"I wouldn't have a clue. I have nothing to do with the build." She looked at the mess. "Or what's left of it."

"Then why are you here?" he asked.

"If you must know, I went and saw Diane. She asked me to look into the project. She believes Reggie's death is related to it. I told her I would check it out. That's all."

Marcus glanced at Lucius. "What do you think?"

Lucius looked over his shoulder and spoke low. "I think you both are asking for trouble. Neither of you should be snooping around here. You might want to take this someplace private. The authorities will be here any moment. Someone is bound to call them. I've stayed too long as well. Christina, welcome back." Lucius turned and slipped out of sight without a sound.

"He's just as sneaky as ever," Chris said.

"I could say the same about you. Let's go." Marcus guided Christina by the elbow out of the area.

"Where are we going?"

"To my office. We're going to have a chat."

"What if I don't want to."

"I have the truth about Reggie's death. Care to hear it?"

Chris glanced back at the rubble, remembering

the blood she had seen before the floors collapsed. "Yes, I think I need to."

"Even if your father is responsible?"

If Marcus thought she would protect the man, he was sorely mistaken. "Especially."

"ARE you sure we can speak freely?" Christina asked as Marcus led her into his office. Being Friday afternoon with no appointments or court appearances, he had given Gloria and the office staff an early weekend.

"Everyone is gone for the day. I sent them home early. But I also had the place swept of electronic ears if that's what you mean."

She took a chair in front of his desk. "It's ridiculous that we have to think that way."

"I'm glad to see you aren't naive to the possibility." Marcus dared her to deny the reach of her family's tentacles. "The question is what are you going to do about it?"

"Me?" Her hands grasped the chair's wooden arms in a death grip. "I didn't come back to Savannah to take over the Morans' business dealings."

"Then why are you here?" Marcus sat on the edge of his desk in front of her. She shrunk back in the chair just enough to show him that she felt her space was being encroached on.

"I'm only here to get something they took from me." She frowned and folded her hands in her lap. She had no plans to elaborate.

Marcus inched closer. "Your family stole from one of their own? I'm shocked."

Christina lifted her face to meet his gaze. "I'm Chris DePalo now. I would appreciate you refraining from calling me a Moran from now on."

"DePalo. Where did that name come from?" Marcus leaned back to give her space to share freely.

"My mother's maiden name."

His tactics worked, and he softened his voice more. "She would have liked that."

Christina dropped her gaze to her lap with a nod. "Unfortunately, it wasn't good enough to keep them out of my life."

Her statement didn't make sense. Had she really fled from her own family? "I want to believe that you separated yourself from the Morans, but I'm struggling with it."

"You mean struggling with the idea of someone leaving their money behind."

Marcus shrugged. "It's a lot of money to say no to."

"Well, I did. I went to New York and started over with nothing but a suitcase and a dream to dance."

Marcus smiled, remembering how dancing had been so important to Christina…*Chris*. "And did you dance?"

"I did a few off-Broadway shows but realized soon that I would make more money in the restaurant business." She smiled so genuinely that Marcus wondered if she had her own tactics to demobilize him. He remembered how her serene smiles and sea-green eyes had a way of making him lose his focus. Was she doing it again? It took him twelve years to get back on track. He couldn't afford another twelve. He finally had the Morans in his clutches.

And they knew it.

"Did your family bring you back here to try and stop me?" he asked, once again leaning forward.

"Yes." Her swift answer took him by surprise. An angry expression flashed on her face just as quickly —anger that felt personally directed at him.

Marcus stood and circled his desk, needing a buffer and a moment to consider his next move. She obviously blamed him for her family tracking her down. He took his chair and leaned back.

"Why do I feel like we've been here before?" he asked.

"Because we have. But that doesn't mean we have to play into their hands this time."

"How do I know you're not playing me right now? I have a legal case that would be destroyed if I trust the wrong person."

"Don't forget you were the one who used me as your pawn last time. If anyone can't be trusted, it's you."

"It wasn't like that," he said, but wasn't able to explain something he didn't understand himself. All Marcus knew was Christina wielded more power than he had believed the day he approached her and asked her out on a date. What started as a play in his mission turned into a conflict of interest the moment that she turned her eyes on him. He'd realized he had met his match.

"Then how was it? Because all I remember is you proving my father right. I was a means to an end for you."

Marcus needed to regain control over this interrogation. She was too close to the truth. "What did your family steal from you?"

She looked away from his face and focused on something on his desk.

He leaned forward but tried not to impose on her space. He was far enough away now. He meant to show sincerity. "You want me to trust you, but you're keeping this from me. How can I believe you?"

"Fine." She paused. "But if I tell you, it remains between us only. It's off the record and can't be used in your case or for any reason. Understand?"

"Okay." This had to be incriminating evidence for her to make such a statement. If it was, he'd find a way to use it without breaking his vow to her now.

She stood and paced his office twice. She folded her arms at her midriff and turned to him. "My brother came to my apartment, but I work nights and wasn't home. My roommate came in and appears to have caught them by surprise. So..." She cleared her throat.

Marcus slowly stood up. "So...what happened, Chris?" He braced for the worst. Was she sharing about a murder? Would she really hide a homicide for her family?

"They took her to get me to come back here. My father knew nothing about Silas's plan, and promised to get her back if..."

Realization settled. Not a homicide but kidnapping for ransom. "Ah, I see. It appears your family is still pulling your strings. That's why you showed up on my stoop. To convince me to drop the suit so you can get your roommate back."

"No one is pulling my strings. I need to rescue Sam. She's got to be petrified. That's all."

"And I need to bring justice for Reggie's death. I won't stop for anyone."

"I understand, but Sam is young."

"I'm sorry about your friend. Though not surprised at Silas's tactics. He belongs in jail."

"Yes, he does." She returned to her seat, and Marcus retook his own to hear her out. "But wouldn't you rather see a criminal case against him?"

"Absolutely. May I call the police and have him picked up right now?"

"He never arrived home. He took Sam to an unknown place and won't return her until you drop the case."

Marcus chuckled. "You're kidding, right? I just told you I won't stop for anyone."

She placed her hands on his desk and stood. "You'll have to if I can prove my family had nothing to do with Reggie's death."

"And after today at the apartment site, I hope you're realizing that you're going to get yourself killed if you keep this up."

"Yes, I thought of that when the floors were falling in around me." Chris closed her eyes and visibly trembled. He knew how she felt. His heart rate had yet to stabilize, and the memory of the sound of the floors crashing still echoed in his head. He wondered how he would live with the traumatic experience but then had to figure it was nothing compared to being in the building.

"And yet, you won't stop?" he asked.

Her eyes opened wide. "I can't. I have no choice. Sam is innocent in all of this. I have to get her back safe and sound. But, Marcus, I really don't believe my family is guilty of killing Reggie."

"Reggie was investigating Moran Construction. And you nearly died on one of their worksites. That's a red flag for me."

"How did Reggie die? You said you had information on his report."

"I have knowledge that it wasn't drowning or suicide. But the medical examiner left it out. Blunt force trauma."

She pressed her lips together and crossed her arms again, this time locked in her thoughts. How he wished he could read minds.

"If I prove someone else killed him, will you drop the case?"

Marcus laughed, thinking she was joking. He sobered at her determined glare. "I can't believe I'm going to say this, but I want to help you prove me wrong."

"You do?" She sounded just as surprised as he felt. "Why would you do that?"

"Because there's already been a death and almost another one today. I'd like to avoid another incident. If that means I consider I'm wrong, then so be it. Either way justice for Reggie will be served. And if someone else is responsible for killing him, then I will make sure they go away for a very long time. But I must ask that if your family is responsible, you won't stand in my way."

Chris reached across the desk for a handshake. Marcus stared at her waiting hand. He wondered why he hesitated to take it. But when he finally made contact, he had his answer.

Christina may have changed her name and address, but the power she had over him remained intact. The fact that he had just agreed to help her disprove his case confirmed it.

CHAPTER 5

CHRIS STEPPED foot out of her hotel and crossed the street to Forsyth Park. She meandered along the walkways, which were draped with live oaks and Spanish moss. Approaching the white fountain that was filled with statues of marble fish spraying water in arches, she circled around the fenced-in fountain and continued by park benches and street musicians.

A man with a flute played a tune, and she stopped to listen to his talented song. After a moment, she tipped him and continued on her way. The sweltering heat had her lifting her hair. Ahead, she saw the stage theater she had spent many nights in. Bypassing the tables and chairs out front, she went inside and immediately felt at home. The ticket counter to her right stood empty since it was so early in the day. The afternoon matinee wouldn't begin for a few hours.

"May I help you?" a voice spoke from behind.

Chris turned to face the man coming out of the office. He immediately recognized her.

"Christina! Where have you been?" He reached his arms out, and she rushed into them.

"Hello, Freddie. I went to New York City and tried to make it on the stage there."

"Tried? That doesn't sound successful." He stepped back but held her hands.

"I'm now the co-owner of a nightclub and restaurant. It's called Club Creare which means "to create" in Italian. My days on the stage are long gone. But that's okay. I'm happy."

Chris looked ahead at the closed doors that led to the auditorium. "I was hoping you would let me take a peek inside for old time's sake."

Freddie stepped back and waved her forward. "Absolutely. Allow me to open the doors for you."

With a grand flourish, Freddie pulled both doors wide and revealed the red carpet and chairs facing the stage at the front. The large platform on the other side of the auditorium beckoned. So many of her shows took place up on this stage.

Chris headed to the left aisle and made her way

slowly down, brushing her fingers along the chairs as she moved closer to her past.

"What was your last show?" Freddie asked from the back.

"*Hello, Dolly!* Right after we closed, I walked home and packed a bag."

"You never said goodbye."

Chris took the first steps to get on the stage. She looked across the auditorium at the man who had given her her start. "Would you have let me go?"

"Never. But after you left, I knew it was for the best. You're not one of them, Christina."

She knew what he was talking about. She never fit in with her family before her mother's death, and it was the start Freddie had given her on this stage that kept her from becoming one of them after.

Chris closed her eyes and pirouetted around the stage, ending with a plie completely from muscle memory.

Freddie clapped slowly. "You still have it, my girl. As graceful as a swan. What can I do to get you to come back?"

"I'm too old now."

"Nonsense! You're just as strong as the last day I saw you."

Chris walked off the stage and retraced her steps

to the back of the house to her old friend. "Thank you for that. I hire musicians and bands for the club, and I love finding new talent. But I didn't know how much I missed sharing my own. There's just not that much work for a ballet dancer on Broadway."

"You're a natural. Have you returned to Savannah to stay?"

"No. I need to return to my life in the city."

"What brought you back now?"

"My family managed to find me and pull me back. They have a lawsuit against them."

"I heard." Freddie led her back out into the lobby and closed the door behind them.

"I was wondering, Freddie, if you knew who my father was using as his foreman for the construction business."

"Sure. Jesse Madigan is now the foreman."

"Jesse? That's surprising."

"Why do you say that? I thought he was always a responsible guy."

"Exactly. He was. But yesterday, I went to the construction site for an apartment complex my father is building and was nearly killed when floors caved in around me. I can't see Jesse approving such carelessness."

Freddie glanced at the glass windows and grew

agitated. "I don't think we should be having this conversation out in the open."

Chris frowned. "Does my father still have such a hold on you?"

"Your father has supported this business for many years."

"So that's a yes. You feel beholden to him?" Chris didn't hide her disappointment at learning her mentor had strings attached to him.

"Sometimes life requires partnerships."

She hesitated to ask the question she always wanted the answer to but did anyway. "Was I even that good? Or did you feel obligated to put me up there?" She nodded toward the stage.

"That wasn't a lie. You are a beautiful dancer."

Chris forced a smile, still not sure if she still got the truth. She stepped up to Freddie and wrapped him in a hug.

"Take care of yourself," he said.

"You too. I hope you know that if it is ever time to go, you can do it."

"Are you sure about that?"

"I did it."

"And yet, you're here still doing their bidding."

"Not for long." Chris held her head high and

walked out the glass doors toward her father's house a block over.

She took the staircase, but this time the door opened for her when she reached the top. One of the men she remembered from the last time held the door for her without a word.

"I'm here to see Vincent," she said.

"You can wait in the dining room. Breakfast is still out if you'd like to help yourself."

With each step, her tennis shoes were silent against the marble floors. She grabbed an apple off the buffet table and took a seat.

"I wasn't expecting you so soon." Her father stepped into the dining room and took his usual seat at the head of the table. "I underestimated your power with Marcus."

"I have no power. I simply made a deal. He's looking into figuring out other possibilities for Reggie's death."

"But the case has not been dropped."

"You know it hasn't. Besides, that wasn't what you asked for. All I had to do was ask him to consider it, and I did. In fact, I went above and beyond by getting him to look elsewhere. Now tell me where Sam is."

Her father folded his hands with his elbows

resting on the arms of his chair. He tilted his balding head as he studied her like a specimen under a microscope. The annoying smirk on his face told her he didn't plan to give her any information about Sam as promised. She knew how he played. He liked to dangle carrots and make it sound as though just one more thing would get her to where she wanted to be.

This would be no different. How could she have forgotten his tactics?

What would his "one more" request be this time?

She took a bite of the apple, trying to act nonchalant while she waited. She couldn't let him see her panic, even while everything inside of her was screaming at the injustice.

"I heard about your mishap at the apartment complex," he said with beady eyes on her. "May I ask what you were doing there?"

Chris struggled to swallow her first bite of the apple. She put it down on the table and wiped her fingers as she searched for her excuse.

"I'm okay in case you were wondering. I wasn't hurt. But thanks for asking." Her sarcasm went unnoticed as her father's face remained unchanged. "I was looking..." She wasn't sure what to tell him. And how foolish of her to think her father didn't have eyes on her. Of course, he would know her every move. "I was just interested in what the family businesses were up to. That's all."

Her father's eyebrows raised for a split second. "I'm glad to hear you say that. I had your room freshened up just in case," he said.

Chris's heart stalled in her chest. "Forget it. I'm not staying here."

"I've asked Silas to bring Sam here. Don't you want to be here when she arrives? I think that might be calming for her to have a familiar face...after all that she's been through."

"Been through? I warned you. There had better not be one scratch on her."

Her father narrowed his dark eyes as she had seen him do many times when he grew angry. "You forget your place, Christina."

Chris lowered her gaze to the apple with one bite out of it, now sitting there looking like Snow White's poisoned apple that she dropped after trusting the wrong person. Chris had entered the enemy's den. What had she expected to happen?

She cleared her throat. "When will Sam be here? I'll make sure I'm here to pick her up." A last-ditch effort to free herself from the Moran clutches.

"This wasn't an invitation, Christina," he said.

"It's time you came home to take your place in the family business."

Never. "That's not possible. Just tell me where Sam is right now. I did as you asked. We had a deal." Panic choked Chris as she realized she had fallen into her father's clutches as easily as Freddie. By doing one thing he asked her to do, she let him know he knew he controlled her still. She might have thought she cut the strings, but her father just proved to her that she had been living a fantasy.

"I'll call the police." She reached for her cell phone, but before she had it out of her back pocket, the man standing at the door swiped it from her hand and smashed it against the wall over the food buffet.

Chris jumped up in shock at the sound, tipping her chair over. "How dare you!" She turned to her father only to see his angry glare. How could she have forgotten about his capabilities? There was a reason she feared him enough to run away in the first place.

He stood with his hands on the edge of the table. He gripped the white linen tablecloth in bunches. "How dare you, Christina, waltzing back in here as if you own the place, making demands when you have no power here any longer."

"I never had power here. Just like Mama!" Her words slipped from her lips without a thought, and she wished she could pull them back in.

Her father's eyes heated to a boil. Then a smile cracked on his face. "Correct. I'm glad to hear you understand that. It will make your stay here that much easier. Something your mother never understood." He nodded once to the man behind her. "Take her to her bedroom."

"Wait!" Chris shouted with her hands up to ward off the man. "I can't stay here. Please!"

The man grabbed her arm and circled it behind her back. Searing pain shot up her arm, and she feared he was about to dislocate it. She cried out in pain and had no way to fight back. All she could do was go with him out of the dining room and up the curved staircase. At the end of the hall, he shoved her inside her old room and pulled the door closed with a slam. In the next second, the sound of the lock clicking over echoed louder than her smashed phone had.

"No!" Chris raced forward and shook the gold doorknob. How foolish she had been to believe herself free. She turned to the two windows only to find them boarded over on the inside.

There would be no way out for her today, perhaps no way out ever again.

MARCUS CALLED Chris for the fifth time in two hours. Her phone continued to go to voicemail, and all he could think was she had set him up. Had he shared anything that would lead to his case being thrown out?

Marcus put his phone in the back pocket of his jeans. He grabbed his car keys and headed out of his townhouse. He needed to know if she had betrayed their agreement. Had she gone to her father already? She seemed so believable, but then she always had. Marcus felt like a fool again. The woman still had him wrapped around her little finger.

Once in his car, he found himself driving to the Moran house and staring up at the windows that had been her bedroom when she lived there. Was she up there now, living in the lap of stolen luxury? Marcus opened his door bent on finding out. But before he could step from his car, his cell phone rang. A quick glance showed it was his brother.

"This is not a good time," Marcus said.

"Actually, it's the perfect time. I see you and what you're about to do."

Marcus looked around the square and up and down the streets. You're watching the Moran house? Or are you watching me?"

"Both. I'm stopping you from making a big mistake."

"Can you tell me if she's in there?"

Lucius was quiet for a moment, giving Marcus the answer to his question.

"Don't go jumping to conclusions. She went in a while ago and hasn't come out. She hasn't been staying here. She's been over at the hotel across from Forsythe Park. That makes me wonder what's keeping her so long now. I wouldn't put it past her father to force her to stay."

"No one forces Chris to do anything. I tried that once. It didn't work."

"I would say Vincent Moran's tactics are a little more dangerous than yours."

Marcus glanced up at the bedroom windows again, this time looking carefully. "There's no light or shadows coming from the bedroom. She hasn't been answering her phone either. Something is definitely up."

"Why do you care?"

"I don't. I'm just concerned that she's ruining my case."

"The only person that's about to ruin your case is you if you walk up to those doors. You have to let this one go, brother."

Let her go. Had he ever really let her go? It felt more like a holding pattern that he'd been in these last twelve years.

"How do you suggest I do that?"

"Start your car and get out of here. Go do something to get your mind off of her. Go to the beach. Go see a show."

Marcus scoffed. "Both of those will just remind me of her. She loved the beach. She loved dancing more."

"Man, you have it bad. But I guess I always knew that."

"*Had* is the right word. *Had* not *have.*"

"Whatever you say," Lucius mumbled.

Marcus sighed and rubbed his forehead. His hand came away wet. The sweat was from the heat, he told himself. Why did it feel like the temperature had surpassed a hundred degrees in a matter of seconds?

"Look, she mentioned her brother kidnapped her roommate from her New York City apartment. I'm just worried that she's turning on me to get her roommate back. That's all. Don't make more of this than that."

"When were you going to tell me that?"

"I just learned about it yesterday. She told me that's why she returned. And that her father was using it to get her to convince me to drop the case."

She told you this, and you think she's a traitor? I'd say she was looking for someone she could confide in. But you just thought the worst of her. Perhaps she's wrong about you."

Lucius was right. How quickly he put his defenses up. "I'll admit that I still have some anger about her leaving without so much as a goodbye. I thought we meant something to each other."

"So did she. But you used her to get to Moran. You can't deny that. I would have left without a goodbye, too."

"I can't change what I did. Yesterday, I had hoped that by making that deal with her, I was proving that I wanted to make amends. I thought she believed me. I thought we could both put our past to rest. But maybe there's just too much water under that bridge."

Marcus started his car.

"It will take more than making a deal with her to get her to trust you again."

"Like what?"

"Well, what did she come down here for?"

"Her roommate."

"Then I would say start there. And if you can track this girl down and prove it was the Morans who kidnapped her, you'll have your case against them and can put them away for a very long time."

"I could get them on murder and kidnapping." Marcus smiled at the thought. "They may not ever see the light of day again."

"And just think how gracious Christina will be to you."

"Chris. She goes by Chris now."

"I know. I looked into her. She's actually quite successful and has a thriving club in the city. Everything seems legit with the business, too. She cut all ties to her family and made it on her own."

Marcus looked back at the house and wondered why she returned then. Would she risk all her achievements for this young girl? Then he thought of the Christina he always knew and had his answer. Yes, she wouldn't have thought twice about helping her roommate. "Moran has something Christian wants back. He must be using that to suck her back in."

"Or she's being held against her wishes."

The idea of Chris being locked up in the house as a prisoner caused a knot to form in Marcus's stomach. He nearly jumped from the car to barge in and find out. But that most likely would get him killed. He knew there were armed guards inside. He wouldn't make it past the entrance.

"If I don't hear from her by the end of the day I'm coming back," Marcus said.

"I'll join you. Until then, stay clean. Let me do the dirty work."

"I'll do my best. But sometimes I'm blinded by vengeance."

"That's why vengeance doesn't belong to you. It belongs to the Lord. Stay focused."

Marcus was surprised at Lucius's quote from the Bible. He didn't think his brother would ever crack that book. More proof that he really didn't know the man. "Thank you for that reminder, Lucius. God does love justice. And He will get it." Marcus looked up at the window again and put his car in Drive. On a sigh, he said, "I just hope she's alive to see it. And to have faith to believe in me again."

CHAPTER 6

CHRIS'S JAIL cell gleamed with expensive golden decor imported from around the world. She knew the white satin feather blanket on the canopy bed was luxurious and comfortable but refused to sit on it. The beauty of her childhood room juxtaposed with the ugliness of her captivity took away all its glamorous appeal. No matter the extravagance, the room was still a jail cell. It always had been, which was why she'd left in the first place.

Chris scanned the space for the cameras that she thought might be around somewhere. Big Brother had to be watching somehow. But perhaps her father just posted a guard outside her door. As sinister as her father acted below, she knew these orders came down from Silas. She cringed at the idea of facing him again but knew it was necessary. For her brother to do this only meant she had something he wanted. He may have even tossed her room for it and now meant to keep her here permanently for it.

But what could she possibly have worth all this trouble?

Chris approached the front window again. No matter how hard she tried to pry the wood away from the frame, it wouldn't budge. Whoever nailed these into the wood made sure to use a hundred nails at least. Even with the right tools, it would take hours to get the boards off. Looking around the room, she saw nothing but frilly pillows and cosmetics.

And her old dancing slippers.

Her pointe shoes with their flat, stiff fronts that kept her on her toes still hung from the mirror of her vanity. As she walked toward them, she caught her reflection in the large mirror and saw the fear in her eyes staring back at her. She reached for the shoes and ran her fingers through the silk ribbons that had seen better days. Frayed at the edges, they resembled her own life. And just as it was with her life, the shoes may look worn, but the construction of them would still help her stand tall.

Chris sat in the chair in front of the mirror and

removed her shoes. She slipped her feet into the slippers and tied them up around her ankles tightly.

She wondered why she hadn't taken them with her to New York. Perhaps, ballet reminded her too much of her past—and too much of her mother. When Chris had reached the city, she never tried out for any kind of ballet part. She went after dancing roles in the various casts but couldn't keep up with the other styles of dance. Perhaps she would have made it if she had stuck to ballet, maybe even tried out for Julliard. She was tall with lean muscle, the perfect ballerina body.

Standing in her room, she found her balance on her toes and lifted her arms above her head. Her reflection in the mirror looked more like her mother than it ever had before. She closed her eyes and imagined a slow ballad and swayed to the music in her head. She had forgotten how free she felt on her toes.

But her toes wouldn't rescue her today, just as they never rescued her mother. Whether Celia DePalo Moran had ever been locked up or not, she most definitely had been a prisoner in this house. Chris wondered how long it took her mother to realize she had married into organized crime. Had she known early on? Had she been in denial? When she figured it out, did she try to leave? Would she have taken her daughter with her?

So many questions that Chris would never have answers to. She always wondered why her mother didn't fight harder when she was diagnosed with cancer. Being locked up in the same house, Chris figured Celia Moran didn't have much to fight for. She simply gave up.

"But I'm not my mother," she said to herself in the mirror. "I will never give up."

A knock on the door had her standing still. She didn't respond but waited to see if anyone would walk in.

They knocked again, and Chris responded, "Who is it?"

"Your father says dinner is ready. I'm to bring you down."

"I'm not eating. But thank you, anyway." Gratitude was missing from her tone.

"I'll give you fifteen minutes to get ready. That is all. The next time I won't ask."

Chris heard his footsteps disappear as he walked away from her door. She had fifteen minutes before he would return. She had no choice but to go wherever she was told. Anger welled up inside of her, and she reached for the lamp on the vanity. Hauling it back, she threw it at the mirror and shattered the glass in spider cracks that fell in a tinkling sound against the wood. Only a few pieces of mirror were left that showed parts of her reflection. Stepping up to it, she realized why she looked more like her mother now. The vacant look of hopelessness reflected on her just as it had when she looked at her mother in her final years.

Chris picked up a large shard and held it in her hand. The piece came to a point at the end. Holding it caused a cut in her palm and she watched a thin line of blood trickle down her wrist. Sitting down, she removed her slippers and ripped the satin ribbons from the back heel. Slowly, she wrapped it around the shard of glass and let her hand get comfortable holding a weapon. The question that remained was would she have enough strength to use it against multiple men. She would only have one chance.

But one chance was all she needed.

Lacing her tennis shoes back up, she found a way to slip the sharp glass into the hem of her pants. She cleaned up the remaining glass and hid it under her bed then waited until another knock came on the door. The fact that no one checked on the sound told her maybe she didn't have a guard at the door, after all.

"I'm ready now," she said and watched the door open to reveal the same goon as before. "When did you start working for my father? I don't remember you."

The man stepped back to let her pass through in front of him. He didn't say a word.

"Okay, nice talk," she said and stepped up to walk him by. "I guess there are many of you goons. I can't know you all. Too bad for you that you got stuck babysitting me." The man fell in behind her, and all she heard was his deep, hot breathing on her neck.

Chris cringed with each step. She took the stairs slowly, considering her next move. Timing would be critical, and she wondered if she should make a run for it as she passed by the front door or wait for another moment of opportunity.

With each step down the staircase, Chris prepared to make her escape. Taking a deep breath, she squared her shoulders and on the last step, feigned a fall, letting out a scream as she went down. Except as she fell, she reached in and grabbed the shard of glass from the hem of her pants and rolled away toward the front door.

Large, beefy hands reached for her as she swung

around with the shard of glass and sliced the man's hand before he touched her.

Shock covered his face as his blood spilled on the white marble. Anger quickly morphed in his dark eyes, but Chris continued to roll until she reached the door and grabbed the handle to pull.

At the same moment, he wrapped his hands around her neck and yanked her back inside. With his hand on her neck, she couldn't scream…but she could kick. Her long leg bent back and hit his kneecap with a crack, causing him to grunt in pain and loosen his hold. She could see out into the square where freedom beckoned. She reached her arms out to try to get a hold of the door jam.

"Help!" She tried to yell, but the sound of her voice was barely a squeak.

Then she saw Lucius in his disguise running her way across the green. *Hurry!* She wanted to shout, but the words wouldn't form on her lips with the chokehold the man behind her had on her neck. Suddenly, the door slammed shut just as Lucius crossed the street.

"No!" She yelled as she felt herself dragged back up the stairs by her neck and hair. Her attempt to escape had failed. There would be no more chances.

Chris wanted to cry from the pain but also from her lack of success.

Then the door flew open, banging against the wall with a crack.

"Let her go!" Lucius shouted with a gun in his hand. He took the stairs two at a time and used the gun to hit the man in the face. Instantly, he caught Chris before she fell and guided her down the stairs as fast as he had entered.

They made it outside before the man and one other who joined him could catch up to them. Chris and Lucius didn't stop running for three blocks. Finally, Lucius guided her into an alley while he stood guard.

"What's going to happen next?" she asked, hearing the desperation in her voice. "I have nowhere to run that they won't find me. I have no one to call who they don't have in their back pocket. All I wanted was to find Sam. Instead, I lost my own freedom."

Lucius hit a few buttons on his cell phone and spoke under his breath. He then pocketed his phone and poked his head out onto the street. "Marcus is on his way. Don't come out until he gets here."

"Where are you going?" Chris realized Lucius was leaving her. "You can't leave me. My father has someone watching me. They'll find me and take me back."

He slipped out without a response, leaving her all alone for whatever happened next, or whoever found her here, cornered with no way out. How could he do such a thing? And how could he think she would remain here like a sitting duck?

MARCUS ZIPPED up and down the grid of streets that made up old Savannah, trying to track the location on the map that Lucius had sent him. He said Chris was at this place, but so far, it felt like he was searching for a needle in a haystack, albeit a very tall one.

He took another turn and was met with construction. Slamming his hand on the steering wheel, he feared he would never find her. It reminded him of another time when he'd hit a dead-end looking for her and how he hated never knowing what happened to her.

"Not again," he said, clenching his jaw with determination. He pulled his car over to the side of the street and jumped out, leaving it behind. He'd cover more ground on his feet.

Holding his phone with the map in front of him, Marcus watched his path get closer to the blinking pin.

Closer to Chris.

And yet, as often as he circled around and as focused as his eyes were, he couldn't see her. Would she have left the spot? Was she taken again?

Marcus called Lucius but only got his voicemail. "Where are you, brother? And where is Chris?" Marcus spoke under his breath in frustration. "What did you do with her?"

Marcus faced the direction of the Moran mansion and took a few steps toward it. He wasn't sure what he planned to do once he got there, but he had no other choice. As he passed by a bookstore located down under an apartment building, he spotted a woman on the other side of the window. She held a book in front of her face, but not her eyes.

Chris's eyes.

He turned and took the stairs to the lower level and opened the door. A bell rang above his head, and the woman lowered the book more when she saw him. It really was her.

"Oh, thank God," he said and rushed forward.

Chris flung the book to the couch and jumped up

to meet his embrace, clinging to him and trembling beneath his hold.

"We can't stay here," she whispered against his ear. "I'm being followed. My father has someone watching me. He knew I was at the apartment complex. He knows I was looking for evidence. He locked me up. If he finds me again…well, I don't want to find out what he'll do."

"Me neither. Let's get out of here." Marcus reached for her hand and held on just as tightly as she did. He led her out of the store and up the stairwell, keeping her close to the brick buildings as he picked up his steps. "My car is a street over. Stay close to me."

They turned the corner, and his car came into view—but so did one of Moran's henchmen.

One man was dressed in a black suit and stood by the driver's door with his hand in his coat pocket, most likely curled around the butt of a gun just waiting to pull it.

Marcus stepped back, pulling Chris with him. "Someone's waiting there. We can't get to it." He racked his brain for another way to get her out of the vicinity. Another man turned the corner and spotted them. He lifted his gun.

"The trolley," she said, jutting her chin toward the

end of the street where a trolley tour was stopped at a pick-up station. She pulled him in the other direction and together they ran, waving their hands to hold the car.

Looking back, the henchmen were now turning the corner, running after them. Both of their guns were out.

"Get low!" Marcus shouted and moved to run behind Chris. They reached the trolley just as it was starting to move and jumped aboard.

The driver chuckled. "What's your rush? Don't you know there's always another trolley coming?"

Marcus withdrew his wallet and tossed a couple of twenty dollar bills at the driver.

"Just drive. Fast," he said.

Then Marcus guided Chris down the aisle until two seats were open beside each other. She took the seat, and he fell in next to her with his gaze glued to the open windows. The gunman had stopped running but was on the phone now.

"They won't give up," Chris whispered. "Someone will get us at the next stop."

Marcus peeled his gaze from the direction of the man to see the fear in Chris's eyes. He brushed the back of his fingers against her pale cheek but had no words to comfort her. She was right. There was nowhere to hide that Moran wouldn't find them. They sat still, staring at each other with no answers. He brought his hand back to hers and turned to watch the road ahead. The next stop at the riverfront was three blocks down.

"Follow me," he said, standing and heading back down the aisle. Chris kept up with him, and as they neared the front, he said to the driver, "We changed our minds. We need to get off right now."

"Here? The stop is right up ahead."

"Yes, now." Marcus took out his wallet and threw a fifty dollar bill on the dash.

The driver stopped abruptly. He grabbed the money, shaking his head and muttering something about tourists. "Not that I'm complaining," he said and opened the door for them.

Marcus was already crossing the street to another block to avoid hearing the rest of the man's complaining. Chris ran with him, doing as he asked, and when they reached two blocks over, he took a turn for the water.

"What are we going to do? Swim?" Chris asked while looking over her shoulder. "I don't want to survive being killed by a brute only to die by water contamination. There's dangerous pollution in this water. Not to mention the alligators!"

"Same here," Marcus said, but he really had no plan once they reached the river. He could be leading Chris to another dead end. But when the water came into view, he noticed the *Georgia Queen* riverboat with its towering red, white, and blue paddle wheel.

"The boat!"

Marcus stopped short. "It's going out already. It just left the dock. This is one ride we won't be catching." Marcus circled the front for another idea.

"I know," Chris said, taking off without him.

Marcus raced up to her. "Where are we going?"

She pointed ahead to a small cluster of yachts moored at the docks. "Out to sea." She turned her radiant smile on him and picked up her speed. "In the lap of luxury."

Stunned, Marcus stopped moving forward. "Chris! You can't steal a boat. That's illegal!"

CHAPTER 7

THE *Pas de Deux* beckoned Chris from its slip along the river. It lined up with other yachts, most of them much larger, but Chris's heart swelled at the sight of her navy-blue hull and name scrawled across the bow. The boat had belonged to her mother, inherited from her father after he passed when Chris was a baby. Chris wondered if the boat had been taken out at all since her mother's death. Chris had no memory of her father caring about the ship, but someone was tending to it. Perhaps her father had sold it, and she was about to steal it from the new owner. She couldn't just walk on board without people noticing.

Pausing on the docks, she turned to Marcus and said, "There's a small dive platform on the boat's aft.

We should be able to board without notice back there. It's low enough and won't require a ladder."

Marcus looked around with obvious concern on his face. "We can't steal a boat, Chris. That will bring in the Navy and who knows who else. I'm not well-versed in maritime law."

"It belonged to my mother. So technically, it's not stealing." She followed his line of focus on the street. At any moment, she expected her father's goons to emerge. She wondered if the person her father had watching her was in the shadows somewhere. "Besides, we don't have much time. Just act like we belong here."

"I've never even driven a boat. If that's even the right term."

"I have. My mother taught me to sail when I was young."

"Like twenty years ago?"

Chris frowned at his reminder of how long it had been since her mother had been part of her life. But his words only strengthened her resolve to take back what belonged to her mother.

What should have been Chris's.

"I hated leaving the *Pas de Deux* behind. It should have been mine in the first place."

"What does it mean? Sorry, I grew up in an

underprivileged neighborhood. I never learned French. And law school is all Latin."

"It means a step for two. It's not a big yacht, but it's comfortable for two. Please, Marcus, come with me. And not because I don't want to break the law alone."

His piercing blue eyes studied her. "Then why?"

Chris glanced down the street, suddenly feeling uneasy for a different reason. "I don't know. After what happened to us the last time, I shouldn't trust you at all, and yet…"

He touched her hand with a mere brush of his fingertips. "And yet what?"

Chris shook her head. "I guess I understand why you had to use me to get to my father. I was a means to the end of his crimes. But now, I could use your help in return. Please, come with me. Consider it restitution."

He flashed her a warm smile. "If I didn't know better, I'd say you take after your father more than I thought."

She laughed. "Is that a yes?"

He frowned but sighed with a nod. "I will live to regret this, but lead the way, Captain."

She took his hand in hers. "Right this way, First Mate."

The two of them walked down the dock, hand-in-hand, looking like just a couple of lovebirds taking a leisurely stroll. When they reached the boat's aft, Chris glanced back up to make sure no one was watching. She put her finger to her lips to tell him not to make a sound. In the next second, she leaned over and grabbed the railing of the dive deck, hoisting herself over as smoothly and gracefully as the whipping wind. The landing of her feet barely made a sound or moved the boat. She gave her nod to Marcus for his turn and stepped out of the way for him to take the leap.

He glanced up the dock, and she wondered if he would change his mind. Then he also grabbed the railing and hopped aboard. However, when his feet hit, he stumbled a bit. Chris reached up to hold him steady, and she found her lips mere inches away from his—a result of being the same height as him.

"You're so tall," he whispered with a smirk. Then his eyes dimmed as he looked at her lips. "Not that I'm complaining."

Chris stepped away from him and ran her palms over her thighs. Her fingers tingled where they had held him so close. "There's no fraternizing aboard ship," she said, trying to lighten the situation.

"I thought this was a boat for two. That sure

sounds romantic to me." A teasing mischief danced in his blues.

Chris rolled her eyes and pivoted on her tiptoes, heading toward the hatch. She lifted the bar to unlock the entrance and climbed through to the dark interior. Instant memories flooded her as she approached the stairwell that led to the deck above and the helm. This was her mother's happy place, and Chris wondered if that was because it was the closest to freedom Celia could ever get. Perhaps she never set sail to escape because she knew her father's hold was strong and his reach long.

Chris waited for Marcus to stand behind her before climbing the first step. He had stopped at the door to the engine room and peered inside where the 10 x 8 black boxes housed the brains of the ship.

Suddenly, the boat jerked and swayed, nearly knocking them off their feet. Chris grabbed the railing to steady herself while Marcus reached for her as well.

"Maybe a boat went by and jostled us," he said.

Then the roar of the engines started, shocking them into silence. Chris looked up the stairwell with her breath stolen from her lungs.

"Marcus, we're not alone. Someone's above deck. It must be owner."

Marcus turned around to head back to the hatch. When he opened the door wide, Chris could see they were no longer at the dock and were heading down the river and out to sea.

She raced forward, but at the door, he put his arm out to stop her. "You can't swim in this water. There are too many dangers that will kill you."

Chris shook her head as she watched the riverfront grow further away. "It didn't kill Reggie. He was killed at the apartment complex. I saw the blood myself."

A confused look crossed Marcus's face. "Why didn't you tell me?" Then a dawning expression filled his eyes. "That's right, you had to protect your father. I'm such a fool. Did you lead me out here to steal a boat to discredit me and my case right from the start? So sneaky of you, *Christina*. I'm going to plead my case with the boat's owner above and hopes he sees how I was tricked."

With that, he turned and headed for the stairs.

"You're wrong. I've done none of these things. Wait. Let me explain."

"I need to get this boat turned around. I have a case to solve. I can't believe I let you make me forget that again. After I had promised never again."

Chris watched him take the steps with angry

footfalls. She wanted to plead her case, but he wasn't wrong. She had kept the information about the blood spatter to herself to allow her father to explain first. She wondered at her loyalty to her father over Marcus. It had been their demise twelve years ago. But seeing how quickly he accused her only reminded her that she couldn't trust anyone.

And maybe Marcus couldn't trust her, either.

Before she could take one step, a loud crash followed by the sound of someone falling on the deck had her scrambling up the stairs. She stepped out of the stairway only to find Marcus sprawled facedown and unconscious in front of her.

She turned around just as something hard hit her head, and darkness took over.

MARCUS GROANED with pain that radiated from the top of his head to every muscle and joint in his body. Ever so slowly, he lifted his chin through the ache and forced his eyes open. Blinding fluorescent light tortured his throbbing head. He waited for the dizziness to abate then turned to his right to see Chris unconscious beside him. Or at least he hoped she was just unconscious.

Marcus dared not speak aloud until he knew who had knocked them out. The boat was still moving, which meant whoever attacked them was now at the helm. Both he and Chris lay on the floor with their hands tied behind their backs, and Marcus wondered what he had planned for them at sea. Thinking about how Reggie's body had been tossed in the water told Marcus it was probably something similar. The farther they made it out, the less likely either he or Chris would return alive.

Marcus rolled along the deck and used his shoulder to push himself up. He watched for any sign of life from Chris and relaxed a bit when he saw her slow breathing. Shimmying over to her, he brushed his cheek against hers.

"Hey, Chris, wake up," he whispered but to no avail. He regretted his last words to her even though his disappointment in her choice to keep him in the dark hurt. He pressed her cheek harder. "You need to wake up. We have to get out of here."

A groan emitted from her lips, and she jerked back away from him. Dazed and confused, she squinted in his direction and then looked around at their surroundings.

"Where am I?"

"Your mother's boat. We climbed aboard, but

someone was above deck and now we are at sea. We have to get off this boat before we're too far from land."

She tried to move her arms and looked down in confusion when she couldn't.

"We're tied up. We're going to have to untie each other. Can you roll over?"

Chris didn't respond for a few moments but then nodded and rolled onto her stomach and then onto her shoulder. Marcus did the same until their backs faced each other.

He found her hands and worked his way to her binds. The ropes were tight, but he managed to loosen one and work it through.

"Ouch," she said.

"Sorry. I didn't mean to pinch you."

"Are you sure about that?" She angled a look over her shoulder as he glanced back at her as well.

"Of course, I didn't." He protested but quickly noticed her teasing eyes. "I guess I deserved that. I'm sorry I got upset with you."

"You should be. Storming off is what put us in this mess."

"True. I should've let you go first." He smiled over his shoulder.

"Ha, ha, very funny."

"But seriously, you should've stayed downstairs," he said.

"I'll remember that the next time I hear you take a fall. Did you see who it was?"

"I was hoping you would tell me." He pulled the last remaining rope from her hands, and she quickly sat up and reached for his.

"All I saw was you spread eagle on the deck. Then nothing but blackness."

A glance over his shoulder showed her trying to work the ropes. "Try to loosen just one. Once you do that, the one next to it should follow."

She bit her lip in concentration and then said, "Finally. I got it." She pulled the long rope free and worked on the next one. Slowly, he felt his hands gain more movement until he broke them apart and rubbed his wrists while he stood up. He pocketed his rope into his pants.

Marcus extended a hand to her to help her to her feet. When she stood in front of him, he reached for her head to feel the bump on the right side. She winced under his touch but let him inspect.

"That's a hefty contusion you got there. I think we have matching ones." He touched his own head as he led the way toward the hatch that would lead to the helm. When he reached it, he put his finger to his lips and motioned that he would open it on the count of three.

At her nod, he used his fingers to count to three, and he pushed it wide for the two of them to run out together.

A man at the controls, quickly let go and put his hands up as he leaned back into the wall. "Don't hurt me!" he said. "I have a right to be here!"

Marcus ran straight for him and grabbed his arms, tossing him into the chair. "Who are you?"

"I'm nobody."

"A squatter?"

"Yeah. That's it." The man nodded his head emphatically.

"You're lying."

Chris stepped up beside Marcus. "I know who he is. I remember you. You're Jesse Madigan. You're the foreman on the apartment complex. What are you doing on this boat?"

"I was told to lay low. Silas said I could use the boat."

"My brother told you to lay low? Does it have something to do with the shutdown of the complex?"

Jesse shrugged and avoided eye contact. "I just follow orders."

Chris stepped closer to the man. She leaned in to capture his attention. "What happened out there?"

The man's jumping eyes flitted between the two of them. "Look, I don't have anything to do with it."

"What happened out there? I saw the blood. You were in charge of the project, so you are involved whether you like it or not." Chris crossed her arms in front of her.

Marcus wanted to ask her how she knew this man was the foreman, but after what happened below deck, he thought it best to let her take the lead and ask the questions.

"I didn't see anything. Honest."

"Stop lying," Marcus said, removing the rope from his pocket. He grabbed the man's arms and brought them around the chair. He noticed the boat was still moving forward with no one at the helm. "Chris, take the wheel. I've got him."

Chris stepped up to the controls and asked, "Where were we going, Jesse? Where were you taking us?"

When the man didn't answer, Marcus pulled the ropes hard to tell him they meant business.

"Okay! We were heading to Tybee Island. I was meeting someone there."

Chris glanced Marcus's way. "Shall we find out who?"

Marcus liked the way she thought, but it could be dangerous. They could be walking into another trap. And yet, they couldn't return to Savannah now. Moran would have his men watching her hotel and Marcus's apartment, as well as his office.

Marcus stepped around the chair to face the man. In his most lethal attorney demeanor, he treated the man as a hostile witness in a cross-examination. "Who are we meeting?"

"You're not meeting anyone. *I* was meeting him. You..." The man swallowed convulsively. "You weren't supposed to make it all the way over. Just her. I was taking you out to sea first."

Marcus caught Chris's shocked expression and knew she understood what Jesse wasn't saying.

The man was going to dump their bodies at sea. Or at least his.

Marcus stood to his full height and towered over the man. "You're not in charge anymore. We are. So tell me, who will be meeting us when we dock?"

Sweat poured from the man's temples, pooling and the collar of his t-shirt. He glanced Chris's way. "I don't want to get involved in any family feud."

Marcus leaned close to the man. "You're already

involved. The moment you hit us over the head and tied us up."

The man shook his head. "I didn't know who you were. I thought you were breaking and entering."

"Then why not call the police?"

"No cops." He shook his head emphatically and looked at Chris again. "But I didn't realize it was her until after I had already knocked her out. That's when I knew I had to get her over to the island."

"Because why?" Marcus's tone left no room for negotiation.

"Because...because I knew that's what he would want. And after the mess up with that lawyer, it's what I had to do to make things right again."

"That lawyer? Do you mean Reggie Brodsky?"

"Yeah, I guess so. He was snooping around the complex. I was told to make him go away."

"Who told you to make him go away? And what did you do?" Marcus thought his head would explode. He knew how to keep his cool in a court of law, but this was too personal. Did this man hold the truth about Reggie's death? Was he responsible for it?

Marcus reached for the man's shirt, fisting it and pulling him forward.

"Ow! You're hurting me!"

"Marcus!" Chris called from the wheel. "You of all people should know a confession under duress will not stand up in the court."

"He knows what happened to Reggie. He knows Reggie did not fall into the river, don't you, Madigan? Now I want answers. Who told you to get rid of him? Was it Vincent Moran?"

The man looked at Chris again. He shook his head. "Her brother," he said nervously. "That's who we're going to see right now. Silas is waiting on the island...for her."

Chris let go of the controls. "He's there now? Does he have Sam with him?"

The man shook his head and tried to shrug. "I don't know anything. I've been hiding out on this boat. I sent everyone home at the worksite and closed it up. Just as I was told to. Moran didn't want anyone scoping out the construction site. He told me to shut it down until he could get back here."

"When did he arrive on the island?" Chris asked. "How long has he been here?"

"As far as I know, just the last couple of days. That's when he contacted me. And I don't know who Sam is."

Marcus interrupted, "I still want to know how you got rid of Reggie?"

"I didn't have to. Someone else killed him. I just dumped him in the river. I found his body at the complex. He was already dead. Like I said, I don't know anything."

"But you did throw his body in the river?"

"Yes."

"And you were dumping mine as well," Marcus asked.

"Far out at sea so another body wouldn't turn up. Silas nearly killed me when the lawyer resurfaced."

Marcus looked for Chris's take on Madigan's excuse. But all she did, was face forward at the controls and pick up speed toward Tybee Island. She had her own questions to be answered and a roommate to rescue. Marcus knew no amount of convincing her would get her to turn this boat around now. Not even the possibility of their deaths.

CHAPTER 8

CHRIS HAD fond memories of Tybee Island. It had been a stop for her and her mother when they took the *Pas de Duex* out, but that was long before she became ill. Chris figured maybe she was sixteen years old the last time they had taken the boat over to the peaceful beaches. Her mother had always dreamed of buying one of the beach houses. The fact that Silas had a place on the island only aggravated Chris more. On top of that, now she was having to rescue her kidnapped roommate from this place of fond memories which tarnished her love for the island—another thing Silas ruined for her.

The island itself was more of a barrier island at the end of the Savannah River. It was known for its wide, sandy beaches with a pier, a pavilion, and various historical ruins of past wars. As Chris navigated by Fort Screven, a guarding fort at the mouth of the Savannah River, she remembered crawling around the gun battery that formerly stored projectiles and gunpowder. She wished she had at least one gun before approaching her brother. Going in empty-handed wasn't the best move she'd ever made. She could only hope the element of surprise would give her the upper hand.

"Where to, Madigan?" she called over her shoulder. "I need some direction."

When the man didn't answer, Marcus pulled on his ropes, and that seemed to remind him who was in charge.

"Just past South Beach," Jesse admitted reluctantly. "He's in the large Italian villa."

"Of course, he is," Chris said, growing more irritated. "Nothing but the best for my big brother. He better be treating Sam well, that's all I have to say."

Marcus asked, "Is there a dock for the boat?"

Jesse replied, "Yes, it's right out front of the house."

As Chris made her way around the island toward the South Beach area, she realized how much she missed this place. Leaving her home in Savannah never bothered her, but leaving this island and its beaches behind felt like she lost a part of her childhood and identity. She steered the boat around the bend until the Italian villa that Madigan had mentioned came into view. The three-story, tan structure was open on the bottom to allow for tropical storms. Currently, there were three black cars parked beneath the house. Her brother always did travel with at least two others in his pack. Like father like son. A glance over her shoulder showed Marcus was also speculating about what they were running into. He captured her gaze, but if he meant to deter her, he held his tongue.

Still, the look in his eyes spoke volumes.

"I know what you're thinking," she said, looking back at the house.

"No, you don't," he replied.

She steered toward the dock. Before she spoke, she noticed Jesse staring at the house in obvious fear for what he believed was his fate at her brother's hand. She whispered to Marcus, "You think I'm foolish for facing him without a weapon or backup."

"I'm your backup."

She stole a quick glance at him, needing to know what he meant by those words. She wanted to believe him, but their past carried more weight. "I was never looking for backup." She spoke from the heart. "I was looking for a partner I could believe in."

Marcus averted his gaze, looking out at the shoreline. She wondered if he would deny his part in their failed relationship. She was glad when he didn't. Instead, all three of them remained somber and silent as she docked the boat in the rolling waves.

The slip felt like a threshold not only to a place of her past but a portal to her future—or lack of one. As soon as she disembarked there would be no going back, not to the sweltering heat of her father's Savannah or the façade of freedom in her New York City life.

"What's the plan, Captain?" Marcus asked.

"To break every hold the Moran family has on me, for good," Chris spoke more to herself. Then she turned to Jesse. "But for now, you are going to disembark first. I know you fear my brother, but if you do as I say, I promise you I will do everything I can to get you out of here alive. Are you willing?"

Jesse nodded once.

"Good. You will walk to the middle of the dock and stop. I want you to lure my brother out of the house."

"What are you going to do?" he asked.

Chris wasn't willing to spill her plans to the man. "I'll join you after. Marcus, you stay aboard and listen to the conversation. Get a feel if Silas is alone, or if he has Sam with him. I don't want him knowing I'm aboard."

Marcus said, "I don't like this one bit, but I'll wait here." He pulled Jesse's wrists. "And I'll hear everything you say. Understand?"

Jesse nodded. "I won't say anything about either of you being here. Promise. Just don't let him kill me."

Chris bit her lower lip in indecision but made up her mind to move forward with the plan. "Okay, untie him." As Marcus worked his binds, she glared at Jesse. "Take your time securing the boat to the dock. Understand?"

Jesse appeared nervous with a sheening sweat on his upper lip. He brought his freed hands to his front, rubbing his wrists. "He's going to ask about you. He's expecting you. What do I say?"

She shrugged. "Tell him you threw us both overboard like you did Reggie. Maybe he'll confess to killing him. Then you'll be off the hook for his murder."

"I told you I didn't kill him."

"Prove it." Marcus moved to face the man. "Otherwise, if you manage to make it out alive today, I'll make sure you go down for murder."

Jesse grew more frustrated, swiping at his hair and yanking it back in a fidgeting grip. He looked at Chris. "Fine. I'll tell him you're swimming with the fish. I'll tell him you fought me, and I had no choice."

"Good. Now, give me your cell phone."

Jesse sighed but turned it over without complaint.

"Both of them." She kept her hand out for the second burner phone she knew the goons kept.

Jesse grumbled something about a death wish but retrieved the other phone from his sock and passed it to her.

Chris waved for him to move toward the hatch that led to the top deck and gangway. "Remember, stop in the middle of the dock to bring Silas to us. Keep him there as long as you can. Maybe show some angst for having to do his dirty work."

"Yeah, yeah, I got it." Jesse may have understood, but he didn't seem too sure of the outcome. But then, neither did Chris. Her brother was unpredictable. She just hoped Jesse could keep Silas busy long enough for her to make her way out through the dive platform and into the house unnoticed.

"Your plan is to swim under the dock?" Marcus watched Chris remove her shoes and place them in a secure dive bag. She hoisted it onto her back.

"My plan is to swim out toward the beach. I'll slip in with the swimmers and exit to the street. I'll come around the front of the house and enter that way."

"I doubt Jesse will be able to hold Silas that long. And what if he has a guard at the front of the house?"

"I'll cross that dock when I get to it."

"Cute, but I'm being serious right now. I think I should go with you."

"So am I. I need to sneak into that house and look for Sam. She's all I can worry about right now." Chris exited the hatch and stepped out onto the dive platform. "If you're joining me, grab a bag for your shoes." In the next second, she slipped into the rolling waves and disappeared under the water.

Marcus watched her emerge ten feet away but stay low in the waves. She moved toward the crowds and quickly slipped in with them unnoticed. He stepped to the right to risk a glance in the direction of the dock, but Silas had yet to exit the house. Marcus worried that this plan would fail from the get-go. What if he didn't come out to meet Jesse? What if he expected Jesse to come to him? Chris could be walking right into danger. Did he really have a choice but to join her? He couldn't let her go in there alone.

Marcus did as Chris said and grabbed a bag for his shoes. Clothed and all, he entered the ocean and follow the same path she had taken. Water pulled and pushed him closer to the shore, but he did his best to stay low and out of sight. He kept glancing toward the house and still no sign of Silas or his men. Marcus searched for Chris and could no longer see her. Then he caught sight of her making her way to the street. She was already so far ahead of him and heading straight into Silas's clutches.

Marcus picked up his speed, not caring who saw him at this point. When he reached the crowds, he rushed toward the shore and up onto the sand in the direction she went. Cutting through a side path, he reached the street and took a left. The summer crowds made it hard for him to track Chris, but he dodged in and out of tourist groups meandering down the sidewalks until he caught a glimpse of her long, wet hair. He'd yet to put his shoes back on but couldn't risk losing her again.

"Chris! Wait!" Calling her did nothing to slow her

down. He picked up his speed and ignored the gawking stares of people watching them both go by fully clothed and drenched. He knew they looked a sight, and the people would never understand the gravity of the situation.

The back of Chris's head came into view again, now closer than she had been before. She was putting her shoes on, and it allowed him to close the gap between them.

"He's not out yet," Marcus said as he neared her. "The plan's not working. He must know something's up."

Chris stood while he put his own shoes on. She glanced up at the house, studying the second and third-floor windows.

"She's up there in one of those rooms. I just know it," she said.

"We should probably call the police and let them go in to look for her."

"I'm not waiting, and Silas would never let them in without a warrant. I'm going with or without you."

Marcus stood. "Of course, you are." He pulled his wet hair out of his face while studying the house on stilts. "Fine. We go in. But through the garage stairs. Not the front door."

Through the open first floor, he could see the yacht and Jesse still on the dock. At some point, Silas would wonder what the man was taking so long for.

Then suddenly the man stepped down from the second-floor deck on the ocean side and walked down the steps to the sand.

Silas wore a pair of tan shorts and an open shirt, whipping in the sea breeze. The wind lifted his shirt just enough to show he had a gun in the back waistband of his shorts. Then two of his men dressed in full black joined him from behind.

"I don't believe it, it's working," Marcus said.

"Let's go. We don't have much time." Chris took off through the first-floor entrance, ducking low alongside the three cars parked beneath the house. She reached the door to the stairwell up into the house, and it opened with ease. "Doesn't look like he's expecting trouble," she whispered.

"Or it's a trap."

She put her finger to her lips and slipped inside, closing the door quietly behind them. Marcus stepped up the stairs first, and when he reached the top, he scanned the open floor plan in a circle. Not a person was in sight, and not a sound could be heard. It appeared they were alone. Nodding to Chris, he ascended the rest of the stairs on careful footing.

Standing beside him, she pointed up to the third floor where the bedrooms must be. The second floor showcased multiple couches and chairs placed in various settings. A large fireplace hearth had two brown leather sofas facing each other in front of it. A large-screen television that took up a whole wall had a sectional sofa set and recliners around it. The television played a movie at a low volume.

Marcus led the way around to the third-floor set of stairs, passing the floor-to-ceiling window that showed Silas and his two men on the dock talking to Jesse. The three men had their arms crossed as Jesse's lips moved fast and his hands moved even faster.

"We don't have much time," he whispered. "Silas doesn't look pleased. And who knows if Jesse isn't telling all."

Chris picked up her pace and took the next set of stairs. At the top, she looked right and then left. She pointed for him to take one way, and she took the other.

Marcus didn't like separating, but he moved to the left side of the house to check the three doors on that side. The first door was a linen closet. The second door was the main bedroom with two walls of windows looking out at the ocean. He caught Silas turning to head back to the house. Marcus ran back to tell Chris it was time to go just as a muffled scream came from the other side of the upstairs.

"Sam, it's okay," Chris shouted. "It's me, Chris. You're okay. You're safe now."

A woman was crying as Marcus ran into a dark bedroom to find Chris struggling to remove a blindfold from Sam's face. The young woman was fighting Chris.

"We have to go right now," he said. "They're coming back inside."

"Wait a minute," Chris said. "Help me untie her feet and hands. Sam, we're here to help you. Don't fight us. And don't make a sound when I take your gag out. Please. They'll kill us all."

Marcus stood at the door, trying to listen for the doors to the deck. "There's no time. Just do her feet. We'll untie her hands outside." Once the men were on the open second floor, there would be no way to escape by them without being seen.

Chris helped the young woman who looked more like a frightened child now. With no time for introductions, Marcus wrapped an arm around her and led her to the stairs at a rapid speed, practically carrying her down the steps. Chris stayed close on his heels, and at the landing, they ran around to the stairs to the first floor just as heavy footfalls and men talking could be heard on the deck.

Marcus took the next stairs with the door to the exit beckoning him to run faster. He glanced back at Chris to see she was still right behind him. They were going to make it. He couldn't believe it.

"Sit down!" Silas's voice demanded, stopping them cold on the stairs. "I'm really disappointed in you, Jesse. You really messed this one up. Your directions were to bring me my sister, not throw her overboard. Now, we're going to have two more bodies washing ashore, and when they're identified, the police will blame my father. We were able to cover up the lawyer and could have made the other lawyer's death be about him being distraught. But my *sister?*" The sound of a gun cocking snapped Chris's eyes wide.

Marcus shook his head as he saw Chris look back up the stairs.

"Go!" she mouthed and waved at the door and turned back.

"No," Marcus whispered, but she was already running back up. Marcus opened the door and whispered to Sam, "Run for the police." He passed her his cell phone and pushed her outside. He slammed the door loudly just as Chris reached the second floor.

"Stop!" she shouted. "Don't shoot him. It's me you want."

But the gun blasted through the house, and all Marcus could see from thirteen steps away was Chris fall backward as though someone had punched her.

No, not someone, but something more powerful —a bullet—had sent her flying to the floor.

CHAPTER 9

CHRIS LAY MOTIONLESS, stunned by the impact the bullet made. She knew it had hit her in the arm and could already feel pain pulsating from her left side. She also knew it could have been so much worse if that man in black hadn't jumped in front of Silas and shot him.

That man.

Who was he?

Everything had happened in a blur. One moment she emerged from down below to see Silas aiming the gun at Jesse, ready to kill him at point-blank range. In the next second, when she called out to him to stop, he swung to kill her. Whether she startled him, or he meant to pull the trigger, she would never know.

She would never know because he was also sprawled on the floor, eyes open with a vacant stare that only meant one thing.

Silas Moran was dead.

But dead at the hands of his own man? How was this possible?

Chris tore her gaze from her brother's face just as Marcus appeared over the top of the stairs, his panicked eyes searching her from head to toe.

"I'm okay," she said. "The bullet just nicked my arm. But Silas…" She looked at her brother again, feeling guilty when elation ran through her. She reminded herself that the man would have killed her without a second thought. Had he been angry at Jesse because he had wanted to do the honors himself?

Marcus knelt beside her, holding her arm, pressing on it to stop the blood flow. Was it worse than she thought? Reaching over to a long table, he pulled down the table runner and wrapped it around her upper arm. "I think that should stop the bleeding. It's not that bad."

"Yeah, I know. Someone stopped Silas from killing me." Chris used her other arm to sit up.

Marcus glanced behind him to see Jesse

inspecting Silas's body. "Where's the other guy?" he asked the man. "I know there were two of them."

"They both ran out on the deck. But everything happened so fast. I guess he could still be in the house, but I thought he went after the shooter." Jesse looked at Chris, a startled expression on his face.

"Well, we're not staying to find out. Let's go." Marcus helped her to her feet and guided her to the top of the stairs.

Chris had yet to take her eyes off her brother. "Wait. Give me a second."

"Chris, I don't think this is a good idea. We need to call the police."

Chris stepped up beside Jesse and looked down at her brother's dead body. As glad as she was that he couldn't hurt her anymore, the idea that he would not have another opportunity to fix his mistakes saddened her.

"He was going to kill me," Jesse said. "After everything I've done for him." He looked at Chris again. "And you stopped him. I wasn't sure if you meant what you said, but you did."

Marcus put his hand across his back, reminding her that they needed to leave. "It's still not safe here. We need to get the law involved. Sam should've already called the police. Until they get here, we need to get outside."

"Sam?" The mention of her roommate's name pulled Chris away from her brother. "Where is she?"

"I sent her out to call for help."

"She was still bound."

"I'm hoping some locals helped her out with that. Let's go find her."

Chris turned for the stairs, but at the top, she looked back at Jesse. The man was a shell of himself now. Realizing that everything about his life had been a lie had to be debilitating.

"Don't go anywhere. I'm sure the police will want to ask you some questions. I'm glad you're alive. You'll get a second chance to make amends. I suggest you start by confessing to dumping Reggie's body." With that, she took the lead down the stairs and out into the sunshine of the sweet island of her memories, thankful that the day's situation hadn't ruined those.

On the street, she spotted Sam, her arms now free, talking to a couple of police officers. As soon as she noticed Chris, she took off running, her arms wide and her facial expression full of gratitude. The police followed her and as Chris enveloped her, she let Marcus fill them in on how everything went down.

"I'm so sorry you were taken," Chris said. "You must have been so scared."

"Is he really dead?"

Chris nodded, and Sam cried into Chris's neck, unable to get any words out now that she had found safety. "I want to go home," she finally managed to whisper.

"Going back to your parents' house might be a good idea for a while, maybe permanently."

Sam shook her head and lifted her face to look at Chris. "No, I want to go back to our apartment. That's my home. With you. Can we go now?"

"Finding you was all that mattered to me. But there's more going on than I understood. I don't think going back to the city is a good idea right now."

"Then where will we go?"

"Not we. You. I'm going to arrange for you to be in a safe place while I make sure nothing like this ever happens again."

"Where am I going? Why can't you go with me?" Sam was visibly panicked with trembling shoulders. As the warm sun disappeared over the horizon, the two of them were both freezing. Chris's clothes had yet to dry, but that had nothing to do with the fear chilling her veins. The loss of blood also contributed.

Chris looked around to make sure nobody was listening. "You're going to Mel's house. She and Jeremy will take care of you. And no one will know where you are. As soon as I get to a phone, I'm calling them to come get you."

"Oh, here." Sam passed Marcus's phone to her. "Use this."

Chris took the phone but chose not to make the call from it. "I don't want to leave any trail to Melody. I'll make the call from a private line. But don't worry. They will come for you right away."

Sam relaxed against her and nodded her agreement. Since Chris's old roommate, Melody married her long-time sweetheart, Jeremy, Sam had a few opportunities to get to know the couple. She had even spent the weekend at their Connecticut home, tucked in the peaceful and secluded hills.

Chris was glad to see Sam accept this next step for her. "Good girl. It's the safest place for you right now."

"I know. I just wish you would come with me."

Marcus left the cluster of police and made his way toward them again. Chris whispered, "Don't talk about this to anyone. But I will join you when it's safe."

Sam watched Marcus. "Even him?"

Chris wished she could say Marcus could be trusted, and maybe he could be. But now was not the time to test those waters, and the least amount of people that knew of where they were going the better, for everyone's sake, including his.

Marcus started talking as he approached. "I told the police everything we know, which isn't much. I mentioned Reggie's death, but until the medical examiner deems his death a homicide, there's not too much interest in connecting today's incident to him."

"I'm sorry," Chris said. "The truth will come out. I don't know how, but I know it will. Maybe Jesse will do the right thing."

"I've asked for a ride back to my law firm. We'll be safe there for the night."

Sam looked at Chris with questioning eyes, waiting to take her direction from her. Chris did her best not to give any of her own plans away.

"That's fine. I appreciate the ride. Even though

Silas is dead, I don't feel comfortable going to my hotel just yet. There are still too many goons walking around the place, and I don't know who will issue their next order. I can't trust anyone."

Marcus frowned and looked at her wrapped arm. "You can trust me. I mean it, Chris. Seeing you fly back like that—" He swallowed convulsively.

Chris reached to tap his forearm. "I'm okay. Whoever stepped in the way, saved my life. For whatever reason, I'm grateful."

An officer stepped up to them, wearing blue latex gloves. "Did either of you happen to see who else was hurt in the building?"

Marcus shook his head and looked at Chris who shrugged. "As far as I know it's just me, and of course my brother. Why? Is there someone else hurt?"

"Whoever ran out onto the deck had also been hit. There are drops of blood down the stairs and into the sand. I'm thinking they took your bullet first before the projectile exited them and came for you."

The idea that one of Silas's goons took her bullet made her wonder even more who it was. They really had saved her life and may lose their own because of it.

Marcus led Chris and Sam into the building of his law firm. He unlocked the first set of doors and then the second set through the vestibule. When he pulled the heavy wooden door open, he saw the lights were on and heard a rustling sound somewhere at the back of the hallway.

"Hello?" he called out.

The rustling sound ceased. In the next second, Gloria peeked her head out from one of the back interview rooms.

"I'm sorry, Marcus. I wasn't expecting you to come in on the weekend."

"Weekend? It's Sunday night. What are you doing here that couldn't wait until morning?"

His receptionist stepped out of the room and made her way down the hallway toward them. Even on the weekend, she dressed efficiently and kept her hair pulled back neatly in a bun.

"Do you ever take a day off?" He made a joke that fell flat. At the moment, he wasn't trusting of anyone, even his most loyal receptionist and assistant.

Gloria walked up behind her desk and took her seat. "I had some filing to get done. You sent us home early on Friday, and I forgot about the Simmons case. You're due in court this week. I hadn't typed up the brief yet."

"Surely that can wait until tomorrow. Go on home." Marcus headed to his office expecting his receptionist to follow orders without question.

Except, she didn't move. In fact, there was obviously something she needed to talk to him about.

"What is it, Gloria?"

She stood slowly and picked an envelope up from her desk. Glancing at Chris and Sam, she said, "I think we need to talk in private."

Marcus looked at Chris and shrugged. "Does this have something to do with a confidential court case?"

She shook her head and shifted her feet nervously. "No, but you may not want this information public."

Chris took Sam by the hand. "We can wait in your office."

As she reached him, he put his hand out and stopped her. "If it's not a confidential case, then just share what you have, Gloria. Whatever you need to say you can say it in front of Chris." He didn't miss the surprise in Chris's eyes at such a remark. But it was the truth, and he needed her to know he never wanted to keep anything from her, not now, not ever.

His receptionist bit her lower lip and then held the envelope out to him. "I didn't open it until this afternoon when I arrived. It was delivered by certified mail on Friday morning, and I completely forgot about it when you sent us home early. I remembered this morning that I never opened it. That's why I came back. It's a registered letter from the county assessor."

"County assessor," Marcus mumbled as he stepped up to retrieve the letter. "Am I being sued by the state?"

Gloria let out a deep breath. "No, sir. You're being foreclosed on. The building is going up for an auction for delinquencies on taxes."

"Delinquencies," Marcus spoke aloud as he read quietly, each word befuddling him further. "I don't understand. Reggie had always assured me the business was taken care of. But this letter claims he hasn't paid taxes for four years?" A glance up at Gloria showed her wringing her hands. "What do you know about this?"

"I've been in the back going through all the internal revenue service forms. There are none for four years. I've looked three times. I tore the place apart." She dropped her gaze to the floor, looking paler than normal. "We have until the end of the month to move out."

"This must be some kind of joke." The words on the page didn't change. No matter how many times Marcus read through them, they reiterated what Gloria said. He had two weeks to move his business elsewhere.

"They're also taking the furniture to offset losses," Gloria said, but he had already read that part. What would he do with a bunch of corporate tables and chairs without a place to put them in?

Marcus felt Chris's hand on his forearm and tore his gaze from the letter. He wasn't sure if he saw sympathy or pity in her eyes.

"Maybe Diane can shed some light on this," Chris said. "She might know if something was going on with her husband."

Marcus agreed and directed Gloria to make the phone call. "Have her come in right away." He turned for his office but looked down the hall toward Reggie's door. He had yet to go in there since his partner's death.

Partner.

The term didn't match his definition of a partner or friend anymore. The man kept secrets from him.

Four years of lying to him, telling him that the business was in the black. He never missed a payment of their profit-sharing arrangement, but he missed paying taxes? Did he not realize they would lose this historic building and be left with nothing?

"I need the key to his office," he said without looking at Gloria. He heard her go through her drawer and remove a jingling ring of keys. She walked them to him and placed them in his hand.

Slowly, Marcus moved toward Reggie's office. At the door, he read his friend's name stenciled on the wood. He unlocked it and went in.

The sparse room matched his own with the same filing cabinet against the wall. Marcus opened it and rifled through past cases his partner had tried. Nothing seemed out of the ordinary, and to anyone looking in the window, it all looked on the up and up. He even had multiple files on the Morans just as Marcus did. Reggie was just as passionate about taking down the organized crime in Savannah as he was.

Except, Reggie's hidden choices mirrored unethical business practices.

Was he one of them? All this time, Marcus couldn't make headway in the least. For over twelve years, the Morans stayed one step ahead of him, if not more. Was he never supposed to gain ground in taking them down? Was Reggie putting roadblocks in his way from the beginning of their partnership?

Was Reggie a mole in the office the whole time? Marcus didn't need to worry about electronic ears listening to his every word if the Morans had real-life ears planted within the walls to begin with.

Marcus pulled out three folders on the Moran family. He dropped them on the desk and sat down in Reggie's chair. He flipped open the first file as Chris stepped into the doorway.

"You might not want to be in here," he said. "You might not like what I find in these files. You and Sam can sleep in my office. There are two sofas in there. I'll stay in here."

She stepped up to the desk and took one look before tapping her fingers on the wood. "You think my father was involved in this?"

"Isn't he always?"

"I can go if that would be better."

"It's not safe for you out there until we know what your father is up to. I know he's behind this tax lien auction as well. I'll be up all night going through these."

"I see nothing has changed." Chris tilted her head

with a frown. "There are other things more important than my father."

"Like what?" He scanned paper after paper, flipping through to find anything with Moran's name associated with the assessor's office.

"How about the fact that I almost died. Do you have any bandages or a first-aid kit?"

Marcus lifted his gaze to the tablecloth still tied around her arm. Both of them still were in damp clothes with mussed saltwater-filled hair. They needed to get cleaned up, and yet he couldn't take a moment away from figuring out what happened to Reggie.

"I don't have much time. I need..." He dropped his head into his hands and stared blindly at the files in front of him. "Need to know if my friend was a traitor."

Out from the side of his eyes, he watched Chris kneel at the edge of his desk. She met him eye to eye and reached for his hand with her good arm.

"He wasn't a traitor. But something must have made him desperate these last four years. Don't jump to conclusions without talking to Diane. His wife will know if there had been something wrong that might lead to this behavior."

"There could be something here that I missed."

"Poring over his files will not bring you answers. He wouldn't have left evidence behind, no matter who was controlling him. You're only causing yourself distress. Don't deny it. I know what I'm looking at…it's the same look you had twelve years ago. The day I left town."

Marcus dropped his other hand to the desk and covered hers. "I hate that he always wins. No matter what I do, Vincent Moran always wins. He even took you from me."

"I ran away on my own."

"He gave you no choice."

"Neither did you."

Marcus ran out of excuses. All he had left was the truth. "I looked for you. I looked for months." He closed his eyes, remembering the dead ends he met with daily. "Nothing consumed me more, nothing besides…"

Chris pressed her lips together and looked at him with expectant eyes. When he didn't finish his sentence, she finished it for him. "Nothing besides trying to take down my father. Don't shut me out. Let me help you this time."

Slowly, Marcus turned in the swivel chair and pulled her toward him. He watched his own hand tremble in hers. He was losing everything that was important to him. And yet, as she placed her palm against his cheek and leaned in to capture his lips, Marcus inhaled at the powerful feeling of a second chance with Christina Moran, the only woman he had ever loved. Suddenly, he realized he wasn't losing everything.

Marcus wrapped his arm around her good side and deepened their kiss, feeling desperate to never let her go again. When he finally broke away and locked his gaze on hers, a mere inch away, he saw something he had never seen before in her eyes.

"I don't deserve your trust," he whispered. "I never earned it."

She touched his cheek again. "I'm choosing to give it to you. Can you say the same?"

Her words were the crux of their problem. The first moment he laid eyes on her and walked up to her to ask her out, he had never trusted her because of her name. Could he let go of his mission to rid the streets of the Moran name long enough to see the individual woman before him? Could he separate her from any connection she had to Vincent Moran?

"I want to. I really do. But I don't know if it's possible. I don't know how to live my life without this need inside of me to make the Moran name disappear from Savannah forever."

"I'm not a Moran anymore."

Marcus huffed, barely smothering a cynical laugh. "Some might call that denial. You're your father's daughter. He knows it, and you know it. You want me to trust you. Start there."

Chris pulled away, and he dropped his hand away from her arm. She stood to her full height, and even though he sat in the chair, she lifted her chin to look down at him further. Did she not realize how it made her look even more like Vincent Moran?

"I'm sorry to hear you say that," she said with disdain. "I had hoped everything we'd been through these past few days would have proven I am not your enemy. That I never was."

"I didn't say you were my enemy."

"You don't see me as part of your team. That's the same thing." Chris turned for the door just as Gloria stepped up.

Strands of hair had escaped from Gloria's bun, and Marcus didn't think he had ever seen her in such a state.

"What is it, Gloria?" he asked. "Or do I not want to know? I'm not sure how much more I can take today."

"Sir, Diane's not answering her phone. And her voicemail box is full. I took the liberty to call the police for a wellness check, under the circumstances with the tax lien."

"And?" Marcus slowly stood to his feet, expecting to hear something devastating had happened to his friend's wife.

"She's gone. All her personal things as well. The house is vacant."

CHAPTER 10

EARLY, the next morning, Chris approached Diane's house and met the officer by the back door. Sam stayed with Gloria at the office until Mel could arrive for her. Marcus now followed from a few paces behind but remained silent since they left his office building. She couldn't believe how quickly things had turned for them last night, and yet, what did she expect? Marcus's hatred for her father was deep-rooted and went back a lot longer than the two of them.

Chris entered the house and stood in the middle of the kitchen. She turned in a circle and noticed the same dirty dishes on the table that were there when she visited Diane just a few days ago. A glance at the counter showed the slip of paper with her phone number scrawled across it. Diane had left it behind. Was it on purpose? Or had someone rushed her out against her will?

Marcus had walked through the house and now reentered the kitchen again. "She left in a hurry, but nothing seems like foul play." He took out his business card and gave it to the police officer. "If you track her down, please call me. She's the wife of my business partner, Reggie Brodsky."

The officer looked at the card and then pocketed it in his shirt pocket below his badge. "I heard about him. Something definitely doesn't feel right about any of this, but perhaps, Mrs. Brodsky just needed to get away from everything. I'll put out a BOLO for the nearby departments to be looking, and I'll contact her next of kin to see if they've heard from her. Do you know if she has family she might have decided to visit?"

Chris waited for Marcus to reply, but all he did was shrug. Then he said, "I'm sorry to say, I'm not positive. She and Reggie spent most holidays with his parents. I could run over there and check with them. Maybe she contacted them to tell them her plans."

The officer nodded and walked them out. "I'll be in touch if I find anything out."

"Same," Marcus said. On the street, he said the Chris, "I'm walking over to pick up my car. Then I'm going back to the old neighborhood to see Reggie's parents."

"The old neighborhood? Where is that?"

Marcus smirked. "A place you've never been."

"Can I go with you?" Chris held her breath as myriad emotions crossed his face. "Please?"

"Why, Chris?"

"Because you think you know everything about me because of where I grew up. I think it's only fair that I know where you grew up too."

Marcus shook his head. She didn't think he would agree. "Don't you have someone coming to pick Sam up?"

"Mel and Jeremy won't be here for a few hours. Sam is safe with Gloria. I have time to go downtown."

"Downtown? You make it sound so sweet like we're going shopping or grabbing a slice of pizza. We'll be going west toward Garden City. These are rough neighborhoods, but they're also people's homes. Most of the residents are doing the best they can to live in these areas of gangs and poverty because it's all they have and ever will have. Something I don't expect you to understand, growing up in your mansion with your gold doorknobs."

"That's not fair." Chris crossed her arms, insulted by his lack of faith in her character. "I gave all that up twelve years ago. Everything I have, I have worked hard for. No one handed me anything. You don't want to be judged based on your past, well neither do I. Let me show you a different side of myself, one that has nothing to do with my family name."

Marcus averted his gaze for a moment. She watched his jaw tick in indecision. "I'll probably live to regret this. But I suppose it could be entertaining. All right, Princess, follow me to the car. Just don't get yourself shot."

Chris bit back a retort at such a reference. After all, she did ask for this. Taking a breath of composure, she fell in line with him but did wonder if she was prepared for this excursion into his past.

Things between them may go from bad to worse. And if guns were going off, the probability of another person stepping in front of a bullet for her was nil.

Marcus drove west into his childhood neighborhood. Chris remained silent beside him as they passed by graffitied fences and rundown homes. He filled the void in the car by acting as a tour guide. "There are nearly seventy sets of gangs on the streets. Most fall under the two largest organizations. But there's also a few others popping up that are all about making a profit. Trafficking guns, mostly, but drugs and human trafficking as well. Most of the sets of gangs are divided by street posses." He jutted his chin at the intersection in front of them. "Like this street here."

Chris sunk a little in her seat. "How can you tell which gang they belong to?"

"Their tattoos will tell their story. Law enforcement does its best to categorize the markings, so they know something about the members they meet, apprehend…or find dead. But the groups are always changing and growing to stay ahead."

"Do the police know which groups are selling the guns? Can't they just focus on them?"

"There's a coalition now with the DA's office. I'm part of it. We're trying to track down the traffickers, but the distribution goes much higher than the street gangs. The suppliers stay clear of the neighborhoods, so they're protected."

"They should have to come down here and see the people they affect." Chris turned away from him and stared out the window as they passed by a cluster of kids in front of a convenience store. "There are even girls in there. None of them look older than thirteen years old."

"They're probably not. And some probably won't make it out of their teens. I pray for them daily." Marcus gripped the steering wheel so tight that his knuckles turned white. "I don't know if God hears me, though. Nothing changes."

Chris turned his way with such sadness in her large eyes. The green in them appeared to liquefy before him. "God hears you, and He sees you too. He sees how you care, and all your efforts don't go unnoticed by Him. But I can understand how you might wonder. When you're in the thick of the darkness, it's hard to not let it affect you." She dropped her gaze to her lap where her hands rested on her knees. "It's hard not to let it consume you and change you."

"Are you speaking from experience?" he asked. "New York City does have its own rough neighborhoods."

"Oh, sure, but that's not what I was talking about.

I was able to find an apartment building with a devoted doorman named Donny."

"Devoted doorman named Donny." He laughed. "Sounds humorous."

Chris frowned. "There was nothing humorous about what my brother and his men did to Donny when they came for me and took Samantha. No, I was talking about the darkness of living with my brother here in Georgia."

Marcus took the next turn to the street Reggie grew up on. He pulled up in front of a multifamily home and parked. He shut down the car and considered his response to her insight into living in the Moran household. As poor as Reggie's home life was, on the other side of the front door was nothing but love.

"He can't hurt you anymore," Marcus whispered but had yet to face her. "Your brother is dead."

After a few moments, he heard Chris sniffle, and a glance her way showed her blonde hair shielding her face from his view. Her shoulders trembled, and Marcus realized he'd neglected to ask her how she felt about Silas's death. He'd just assumed she wouldn't be affected by it after all the man had done.

He'd assumed wrong.

"Hey, I'm sorry," Marcus said, reaching for one of her hands to hold. "That was blunt and uncalled for. I'm sure you had hoped someday Silas would change. I think I've seen too much death down here to be cynical about people changing. Those junior high schoolers back there most likely won't. They're in it to the end. Whatever that end happens to be for them. I'm numb to it, but you're not. I should have realized that."

Chris shook her head and lifted her reddened eyes to him. "Silas knew the kind of life he lived. I'm not naïve to why he died by a gun. He lived by the gun. And he almost killed me today because of it. I'm sad because I thought I had escaped this darkness, but I see that darkness pulls you back in if you let your guard down. I let my guard down. When my father hears that Silas is dead, he will be relentless. All he talked about was me returning to take over the family businesses. Marcus, I may never be free again."

So much was on his tongue about some of those Moran businesses. But now was not the time. Right now, he needed to be honest with Chris on a different topic.

"You're stronger than you give yourself credit for," he said. "In fact, if I played any part in causing you to doubt your strength, I am sorry. The truth is I envied you when you were able to walk away from your darkness. I am consumed by mine. It's all I can focus on. It has me in its grip. But not you. I know you're afraid your father will have the power to control you, but I don't see you ever giving that up."

She tilted her head and looked at him with an unconvinced expression. "If it wasn't for your brother, I would still be locked in my room."

Marcus rolled his eyes. "Just great. Now I have another favor I owe him. Will it ever end?"

Chris giggled so sweetly that the sound made him smile. "Well, he did leave me in an alley with a gunman chasing me."

"Right. Never mind. I owe him nothing. Phew."

They shared a laugh that trailed off into silence. Chris looked away to face the house outside of her window.

"So this is where Reggie grew up?"

"Yes, and mine was the house two doors down. The second-floor unit. My parents are not there any longer. I moved them out after I joined the practice."

"But Reggie's family remained here? Why's that?"

"They didn't want to move. Mrs. Brodsky said this neighborhood was all she knew and would never give up hope of seeing it rehabilitated."

Chris hummed. "Talk about a strong woman."

She pulled the door handle. "I'm excited to meet her."

"Wait," Marcus said, jumping from his side of the car. He raced around the front and opened her door.

"Marcus, I can open my own door." She stepped out without taking his hand.

He wrapped an arm around her back. "Humor me. I've already seen you take a bullet once this week."

Chris pressed closer to him and glanced over her shoulder. "If you're trying to scare me, it's working."

"If scaring you makes you want to be this close to me, get ready to be terrified constantly."

Marcus felt her shoulders rumble with laughter, but he was glad she didn't pull away. He liked her right where she was. Together they walked up the stoop to the porch of his friend's house. He had just been here to inform them about Reggie's death, and now he was here to ask about Diane's disappearance. How much more bad news could the family take?

He rapped on the door and was greeted by the sound of their German Shepherd barking. Soon, the curtain lifted from the window beside it, and the lock turned over.

Martha Brodsky clapped her hands in delight after opening the door for them. "Come in, Marcus, welcome back." She stood on tippytoes to kiss his cheek. Then she gasped at the sight of Chris. "Christina Moran, I don't believe my eyes. Is this your first time on this side of the tracks?"

"Martha, be nice," Marcus warned, even though he knew the woman was joking. He couldn't really blame her. He never dared bring Chris to his hometown when they were dating.

Martha reached for Chris and gave her a hug. "I'm just kidding. Welcome to my home. You just couldn't stay away from beautiful Savannah, could you? I completely understand."

Chris glanced over Martha's shoulder at him. Her eyes were wide with surprise. "Actually, it wasn't my choice to return, but yes, Savannah will always hold a special place in my heart."

Martha pulled away and patted her cheek. "Follow your heart. You'll never regret it." She led them into the living room. Old but sturdy and well-maintained furniture welcomed them. The rooms were meticulously clean, proving cleanliness was a priority for the Brodsky family. The state of the neighborhood outside didn't affect the inside of their home.

"Can I pour you some sweet tea?" Martha asked, turning toward the stairs to the second floor. "Joe!

Marcus is here with his girlfriend! Hurry up and get down here! I'll be right back with your iced tea. Make yourselves comfortable."

Once they were alone, Marcus whispered, "Sorry about that. She means well."

Chris smiled, a slight pink blush on her cheeks. Did she even know how beautiful she was? "I understand she didn't mean anything by calling me your girlfriend. I'm surprised she remembered me at all. I'm embarrassed to say I don't remember meeting her."

"You didn't."

Chris tilted her head in confusion. "Then how does she know me?"

"Everyone knows the famous Moran heir."

Chris frowned as Joe Brodsky trudged down the stairs. "Well, well, look what the ferry boat dragged in. Christina Moran." Joe took her hands and kissed the backs of them, first one then the other. "To what do we own this honor?"

Chris glanced in terror at Marcus, the words "help me" practically on her lips.

Marcus smiled and saved her from any more embarrassment. "Mr. Brodsky, we're here to ask you if you've heard from Diane. It seems she left town recently but didn't tell anyone."

"I don't think so." Joe rubbed his bald head. Just then, Martha stepped into the room with a tray filled with four glasses of sweet tea. Joe continued, "Honey, have you heard from Di?"

"Not in a week. I left her numerous messages. I planned to drive over tomorrow if she didn't return my calls. Why? What's going on? Is she okay? I've been worried about her, no matter how many times she says she's fine. She just lost her husband, *my* son. How can she be fine?"

Martha passed out the teas and took her seat beside Chris on the sofa. She sipped her tea, sweet enjoyment on her lips. Then she noticed the somber look on Chris's face.

"Why isn't anyone drinking their tea? What happened?" Martha straightened in her seat.

Marcus had no other way to say this but to just say it. "The state is taking the law building from me. Apparently, Reggie hadn't been paying the taxes for the last four years. I need to find Diane to see what she knows. Are you sure you don't know where she might have gone?"

Martha sat stunned and silent. Slowly, she put her tea down on the tray. She pursed her lips, and all the warm welcome left her. "Now you sound like

Diane. I'll tell you the same thing I told her. My Reggie would never steal. He was honorable."

Marcus leaned in, confused by her words. "What do you mean? Did Diane come to you about this? Did she know about it before Reggie died?"

Joe put his hand on his wife's knee. "Don't raise your blood pressure, dear. Marcus is not the enemy."

Martha stole a quick heated glance at Chris. "Marcus isn't, but she is."

Chris was about to stand up, but Marcus shook his head for her to remain seated. Thankfully, she gave him a moment. "Chris is not our enemy. I promise you that. I wouldn't have brought her here if I thought so. You can trust her. Please, tell us what you know."

Martha released her anger, and after a moment said, "I'm sorry, Christina. That was unfair of me. I shouldn't judge."

"It's okay," Chris said. "Maybe I deserve your criticism. I was a bit clueless when I lived in Georgia. But you can trust me now."

Diane came by a week before Reggie disappeared. She had a foreclosure notice on the house. They were losing it. So, I'm not surprised about the law firm building being taken. I'm sorry, Marcus. This must be killing you."

"That's an understatement," he mumbled and looked at the floor. He felt Chris touch his hand, and he quickly held on. "So Diane knew Reggie was struggling. You knew he wasn't paying the taxes and mortgage on his home. Why wasn't I told? I was his partner. I was his friend."

Martha smiled sadly. "His very best friend, sweetie. He looked up to you and wished he was as brave as you. He let you battle the court cases because he knew he could never do them justice. Not like you." She glanced at her husband and at his nod, she continued, "But Reggie hadn't always been so honorable. He took hush money for a long time. It's how he had the money to buy the house and business in the first place. But when he tried to break free and do the right thing..." She sighed and dropped her head. "Well, they broke *him* instead."

"Who is they?" Chris asked and then inhaled sharply. "On second thought. Don't answer that. I already know the answer." Chris stood and headed for the door. She stopped with her hand on the doorknob. "Marcus, take me home."

"Home?" Marcus asked, slowly gaining his feet.

"Yes, home. I want to see my father's face when I tell him his legacy has come to an end."

CHAPTER 11

MARCUS ENTERED the Historic Savannah streets, driving toward the Moran house. "I don't think you should go in." He spoke his mind, even though he didn't think Chris would listen. Her anger was heavy and seething in the car, and he feared for her safety if she made an irrational move. However, seeing this angry side of her, he also feared *her* a little. Maybe he was underestimating her.

"My father will have been notified about Silas by now."

"I'm sure. He may take his pain out on you. If he locked you up when he wasn't angry, I don't want to imagine what he'll do now."

"He needs to be stopped, and I am the only one left to do it. His reach has touched everyone I have loved and cared about. I'm surprised he has nothing on you."

Marcus reflected on her comment for a moment. He drove in silence as he wondered why Vincent Moran left him alone. He got to Reggie, so why not him?

"Maybe Reggie made a deal with him," he said, thinking aloud. "Maybe my partner sacrificed himself to keep me clean. He knew I was the relentless litigator between us. He was the businessman. Maybe I was part of a transaction."

"Except, Reggie had been delinquent on taxes for four years. If the bribe money to my father stopped four years ago, you would have heard from him by now. So something else kept him from showing up on your doorstep."

"Maybe he couldn't find anything on me. The fact that his only connection to me was you tells me that I'm untouchable to him."

Chris scoffed. "No one is untouchable. We all have skeletons in our closet. Things we have done that we wished we hadn't. He would have dug until he found something on you. Something from your past in your neighborhood, perhaps. Can you honestly tell me you have never done anything wrong? Nobody's perfect. We all fall short. God's word tells us that. So be honest."

The temperature in the car seemed to skyrocket, and it had nothing to do with the summer heat. Marcus drove in silence as a few memories resurfaced from his college days. He had some things he wished he could forget or go back and change.

"Okay, I'll be honest. I broke some rules to get out of my neighborhood. I was a different person then. Law school changed me. But Jesus transformed me. I suppose I don't think of those days anymore because I do my best to walk with God daily now."

Chris smiled softly beside him. "I'm really glad to hear you say that, Marcus."

He glanced away, a little embarrassed at his quick confession of his faith. "Why? Because I'm going to need Him more than ever now?"

"We always need Him." She slapped her hands on her knees. "But yes, if it was Reggie keeping my father at bay, you can expect him to start digging up everything you don't want people to know about you. He may even come in as your rescuer to save your firm."

Marcus felt his jaw drop. "Reggie's not even in the grave yet. That would be cruel."

Chris raised her eyebrows. "Have you met my father?"

"Actually, no, I have never met Vincent Moran. At least not formally. I've hated him my whole life and wouldn't have put myself in a situation where I would have to be in the room with him."

"Why would a boy from the west side care about my father?" Chris's eyes narrowed at him with genuine curiosity.

But could he tell her what he knew?

"Chris, you say I can trust you, right?

She hesitated for a second. "Yes, and I meant that. I will hold your confidence in whatever you have to tell me."

"It's not about holding confidence. It's about me being able to trust that you won't try to interfere. You could get yourself killed with this knowledge."

As Chris sat in contemplative silence, Marcus took the next few turns and parked at the end of the street, choosing to stay clear of the Moran house. When she didn't step out, he wondered if she had changed her mind.

"You don't have to go in," he said.

"Tell me what you know."

"Are you sure? I watched you leave the Brodsky house in a rage of fury. You won't be able to do that with this information. Instead, it will consume you and depress you because it's a battle that can never be won. The coalition tries, but there are even days that I wonder if Moran hasn't already gotten to them."

"Tell me," she said again. But she had yet to look at him. She faced forward with her chin held high, an invisible shield around her as she waited for his words to hit her. She was already braced for impact.

All that was left was his decision to share or not.

As soon as the words were out, there would be no going back. "Give me your hand," he said, holding out his own.

"So you can hold me here. That will make you no different than my father. He kept me locked in my bedroom because he knew I would leave. You either trust me to stay or you don't."

Marcus moved his hand to the steering wheel, wrapping his fingers around it for his own stability. He had to trust that she wouldn't react irrationally and undo all the work that he and the coalition had already done.

"All right, the truth is the Moran family has been supplying guns to the gangs on the Savannah streets."

Chris's eyes grew wide. "What?" She looked

straight at him with as much shock in her expression as he had hoped to see. It meant she knew nothing about it and had never been involved in any way. The one good thing Vincent Moran did was protect his daughter from his involvement in his crimes.

"I know it's hard to comprehend. The idea of someone putting guns in kids' hands is too insane to understand and feels like something that only happens in the movies. But this is real life. The gangs get the guns from someone."

"That someone doesn't have to be my father." She glanced at the house, a place full of wealth and prominent status. "How would it benefit him to keep crime up?"

"Crime affects business. It affects real estate prices. Most people would want lower crime and higher real estate. Unless, of course, you're the one looking for cheap land to build slum housing."

Chris leaned back on the headrest and stared at the ceiling. "Of course. He has never been interested in philanthropy unless there was an angle to play. Do you remember Freddie from the theater?"

Marcus wondered about the change of topic but nodded. "Sure, Freddie's been working there for years. Why?"

"I went to see him and realized my father has

something on him too. He's just a man who runs a theater. My father doesn't even care about the shows. He never attended any of mine. So why invest in Freddie's business unless he can use Freddie to lift his own business up." She turned to face him. "At the end of the day, it's all about his bottom line. It doesn't matter who had to die that day or go to jail. Loss doesn't matter to him because he has others lined up to take their place. He has a machine so well-oiled that he can sit up in that house and never lift a finger to do any work, dirty or otherwise. And because of that, he's untouchable. It's not fair."

"Life isn't fair, believe me. Laws are put in place to protect people at the same time other laws are created to protect the criminals. Deals are made for lesser sentences for career criminals while those who spend their lives trying to do the right thing get the book thrown at them when they slip up once. I take solace in knowing that there will be a true judgment day someday. Real justice will be served by the One who avenges for us."

Chris closed her eyes. "I just keep seeing those kids from your neighborhood. I have to believe that God will avenge them too."

"He will. He promises that anyone who has

caused a child to stumble or harmed them in any way will be punished. That it would be better for them to have a millstone tied around their neck and thrown into the sea."

Chris laughed nervously. "If that would be better for them, I would hate to see what their actual punishment will be." She sighed and now reached for his hand. "I work so hard to keep girls off the street. I can't save them all, but when I see one that needs to believe someone cares about them, I do my best to give them a place to live or give them a job. To think that my father is doing just the opposite kills me. I don't know if I can wait for God's justice to be served to him."

Marcus rubbed her hand with his thumb. "This is why I worried about telling you. You can't do anything or say anything. The coalition is trying its best to catch him. If we can, we will put him away and anyone else who has worked for him. I can't have you alert him. Do you understand?"

"I understand. I don't like it, but I understand. I think it's best if I don't go in there right now. I may not be able to control myself. Just go back to Gloria's. Mel and Jeremy should be arriving soon if they're not already there."

Marcus refrained from showing relief and put the car in Drive. He continued the rest of the way down the street, slowly creeping by the Moran house to his left. Suddenly the front door opened, and he picked up his speed so he wouldn't be seen.

"Wait." Chris grabbed the wheel. "Is that your brother?"

Marcus slammed on the brakes just as Lucius came down the front steps. Lucius also halted, freezing in his spot. This time he wore no disguise. Just a ponytail and a black sport coat and black pants—looking like a Moran henchman.

The two brothers stared at each other, both in shock and horror.

In the next second, Lucius pivoted on a run, but not before Marcus noticed a large bandage on his hand.

Marcus hit the gas, but by the time he made it to the corner, his brother had slipped into the shadows once again.

CHRIS COULDN'T IMAGINE how Marcus must be feeling. Everything he believed his life was about was coming unglued at the seams. His business was over. His coalition was proving to be useless. Reggie, his friend and business partner, was dead, most likely murdered. And now, his brother, his own twin was working for the enemy.

Lucius Cartwright was one of her father's goons.

As they returned to Gloria's apartment, Marcus pulled up to the door and said, "I'll be back in a little while."

Chris had her hand on the door handle and paused. "Where are you going?"

"I'm not sure. Maybe the firm. I just need a quiet place to process this."

"Are you sure you're not going looking for him? You asked me to refrain from reacting to the information you had about my father. I'm asking the same of you."

Marcus shook his head. "I'm not going after him. He wouldn't tell me anything anyway. I honestly have no idea what my brother does for a living. It's always been a big secret since he got out of the military. But seeing him step so casually out of the Moran house tells me it wasn't his first time going in and out. There was also a day when I was going to meet you there, and he called me before I got out of my car. He was there watching me. I thought he was watching the house, but perhaps he was watching from the house. He hinted that you had been taken but told me to go home. Unreal."

Chris could tell Marcus was struggling to understand this information. "Rehashing every conversation that you've had with Lucius won't help you. The man lives in disguise, and that means his words are just as…"

"It's okay. You can say it. A lie. His words are all lies."

Chris sighed. "That's not what I was going to say. I was going to say fake. I don't think Lucius means to lie to you. He's your brother, and he loves you. That much I know is true. He must have a valid reason for working for my father. If nothing else, he did rescue me from that house. Focus on that. I probably would be dead if he hadn't shown up and burst in. I had just cut the guard with a piece of glass. He was ready to kill me, or at least pummel me. I, for one, want to give him a chance to explain. I owe him that."

Marcus blew out a deep breath. "I'll remind myself of that when I see him."

"So that *is* where you're going. You're going to look for Lucius."

"I have to." He nodded to Gloria's apartment. "I want you to stay here with your friends. No one knows you're here, so you'll be safe."

"My brother is dead. There is no one else after me to kill me."

"Still, humor me. Your father may decide to carry out Silas's plan. In fact, you might want to go back with your friends to Connecticut. You'll be even safer there. What could possibly go wrong in a small country town?"

Chris giggled despite the heavy conversation. "Actually, before Jeremy and Mel married, they both had to fight a killer in that small country town. They nearly lost their lives and each other."

"I'm sorry to hear that. Living in the city my whole life, I suppose, I always thought the grass wasn't only greener but sweeter on the other side of the buildings. The attorney in me knows that crime can happen anywhere. But for the most part, it typically is a lot tamer. Maybe someday I'll hang my shingle in a little country town and work on probate cases." He chuckled.

Chris rolled her eyes. "You would be bored out of your mind, and you know it. No, Marcus, God has you here for a reason. You love Savannah, and you will fight for it until your dying breath."

He flashed her his beautiful smile, and she knew she was right. Marcus Cartwright may have lost his building, but he would rebuild his business again right here in Savannah.

"I need this place just as much as it needs me," he said proudly.

Chris opened the door and stepped out. Glancing back inside, she said. "Don't be too long. I would love for you to meet Mel and Jeremy. Mel was the first girl I rescued."

His eyes dimmed as did his smile. "Sounds like New York City needs you too."

Chris agreed wholeheartedly. "I suppose I am a city girl at heart. I've never cared much about the grass. I'll say good night, but I won't say goodbye. Good night, Marcus." She shut the door and headed into Gloria's apartment.

Chris wasn't inside for more than two seconds before she found herself embraced by her best friend of more than ten years. Mel Styles, formally Mel Mesini barely came up to her neck, which was fine, because Chris loved to use her soft, brown curls as a place to rest her chin.

"I need to get you another cell phone. I don't like not being able to call you," Mel said, squeezing her tighter. "Thank God you're safe. Sam filled us in on what has been happening." She pulled back and looked up at Chris. "I had no idea the danger you ran from. You hid it well, my friend, but you shouldn't have."

Jeremy stepped into the kitchen. He wore civilian clothes, but his serious cop expression was in place. His blue eyes held no warmth as he looked at her bandaged arm. "Is it safe for us to be here, Chris?"

Chris let go of his wife and nodded. "For now, but I still want you to take Sam back with you. I'll come for her as soon as I can."

Mel looped her arm through hers. "Please come with us now. There's no reason for you to stay."

A flash of Marcus's face crossed Chris's mind, but she pushed that thought away as ludicrous. She needed to focus on her future, not her past. "I need to end things with my father, or I'll never stop looking over my shoulder. I shouldn't have in the first place. I got too comfortable, lazy even."

Jeremy said, "I'm sorry you're going through this, but you put lives at risk by not being honest. Poor Sam is traumatized." He pulled his wife close to him and kissed her forehead. "It could have been Melody that they kidnapped if your father decided to come for you two years sooner."

Mel shushed her husband. "That's not helping, Jeremy. Chris did what she thought was best."

"She kept you, Rafe, and Sam in the dark."

There was no reason to deny Jeremy's words. "No, Mel, he's right. I put you all at risk. All I wanted was to help you and give you a safe place to fall. You were a runaway just like me. I wanted to give you what I wished someone had given me. I was hurt and broken and scared. I thought if I believed in you and helped you then I was better than the family I came from. I was living a lie."

Mel pulled away from her husband and took Chris's hands. Her liquid brown eyes shimmered with tears. "I have told you before, but I will tell you again. You saved my life. Please, Chris, let me return the favor and take you back with us. We can leave tonight. We don't have to wait until the morning. And you'll never have to come back here again."

"And what, change my name again? Move to another apartment? To another city? I'm tired. I don't want to start over. And…"

"And what?" Mel prodded her to continue.

"You're going to think I'm crazy, but I want to see my father ruined."

Jeremy folded his arms at his chest. "Are you

talking about physically harming him? As a police officer, I must counsel you against that."

Chris shook her head. "No, I don't mean violence. That's *his* MO. I mean I want to see him lose everything. His power, his money, his reach. I want to see it all cut off. And if I go back into hiding, he wins and all those things just multiply."

Mel glanced over her shoulder at her husband. Jeremy nodded to her and pulled her close into his chest again. "I'll be praying for you nonstop. You can trust that Sam will be safe with us, and if you change your mind, you know where we are. But you have to promise me something."

"What's that?"

Mel dropped her hand to her belly. "That my little baby will meet her aunt."

Chris inhaled sharply while tears filled her eyes. "You're having a baby?" Her voice squeaked. "Why didn't you tell me sooner?"

"We planned to when we came into the city next week. I wanted to tell you in person. You have to come back to us. Promise me you will."

Chris reached for her friend again. "Of course, I will." But even she detected the lack of surety in her voice. She glanced over Mel's head at Jeremy and mouthed, "Take care of her."

He mouthed back, "Always."

Taking a deep breath, she composed herself and pulled back with the most excited smile she could muster for her friend. "When are you due? Let's go into the living room and talk. You have so much to tell me. So, you're having a girl?"

"Well, it's too soon to know, but we have heard the heartbeat. She's going to be so strong."

Jeremy cleared his throat, sitting across from them in the recliner.

"Okay, maybe he," Mel corrected herself with a wink toward her husband.

"Oh, Jeremy, who are you kidding?" Chris teased. "You would spoil a little girl rotten. And make sure all the boys stayed away until she is eighteen years old."

"True that," he replied without hesitation.

Mel put her finger on her chin. "Speaking of boys, would you care to share about who this Marcus is? He is all Sam is talking about."

Chris waved her hand. "He's just someone I used to know."

Mel's mouth dropped wide. "I don't believe my eyes. The always cool and collected Chris DePalo is blushing. Jeremy, go to bed. Chris and I have important girl things to talk about."

"I said there's nothing to talk about. He's nobody." Chris shifted uneasily on the sofa. As Jeremy stood up to leave, she said, "You don't have to go anywhere. Save me, please, Jeremy!"

Jeremy didn't even look back. He just walked upstairs. Halfway up, he said, "I consider this justice served. Good night, Chris, although for you, I think it's going to be a very long one. Enjoy the hot seat."

CHAPTER 12

Marcus sat at his desk with his hands folded on top. The only light on in the dark building was the small lamp off to his right. He hadn't moved since he arrived over an hour ago. Chris had asked him not to go after Lucius, but she didn't know that no one ever went after Lucius. His brother always came to them. And tonight would be no different.

"How long have you been working both sides?" Marcus asked into the shadows. He couldn't see his brother but knew he was there somewhere, hidden as always.

"Don't ask questions when you're not ready for the answer." The response came slow and smooth. If his brother was ruffled at all, he hid his emotions well.

"I would say at this point I have nothing left to lose. If your plan was to break me as you broke Reggie, then I would say you succeeded." Marcus looked around his office. "I have a matter of days before I must be out of here and have no place to go and no money to start again. My whole career has been a façade. A lie, and you knew it. The least you can do is step into the light to face me."

After a moment of silence, the floor outside his office door creaked. Then Lucius stood in the doorway, still shadowed but out in the open now. Marcus noticed the bandage on his hand again.

"It was you," he said. "You killed Silas and took the bullet meant for Chris. Why?"

"I can't tell you. It's part of—"

"Your job, yes, I've heard that before. Many times. And yet, I have no idea what this job that you do is all about. I have no idea if it even exists outside your head. Who do you work for? And don't say Vincent Moran, because you just killed his son. Does he know it was you?"

"Absolutely not. And you will not tell him, or you will jeopardize something so much bigger than the Moran family. That man is chump change, but even he doesn't realize it. This goes way beyond Savannah, and as I told you last week, if you keep this up, you will be killed."

"Who...do...you *work for*?" Marcus shouted, slamming his fist on the desk.

Lucius looked to the ceiling and then took a step inside the room. First one, then another until he stood fully in the lamplight.

All disguises were gone, and it was like looking in a mirror. This twin of his had cut his hair and lost any sign of the beard, the fake one and the real one.

He even wore a suit.

Marcus smirked. "I thought you wouldn't be caught dead in a suit? Or is the Moran black suit your one exception?"

"You need to leave town...tonight," Lucius said in a low demanding voice. "I'm going to finish this. Don't come back until you hear that Vincent Moran is dead."

Marcus leaned back in his chair. "Are you confessing to me, a man of law, your plan to kill someone? Premeditated murder will get you 25 to life. In case you didn't know capital punishment is a legal penalty in the state of Georgia. With my testimony, you could be looking at the death penalty."

Then the disguise became clear.

He nearly bent over as though his brother physically punched him. Marcus felt his heart pound practically out of his chest. Air seized in his lungs and choked him. Never had he felt so deflated...so disappointed. "You traitor. You want me to leave town so you can frame me for murder. Of course." Marcus huffed. "And here I thought you were out of disguise, but brother, this getup is your grandest incognito yet. Well done." Marcus slow clapped. "Growing up, I never let my guard down in case someone slipped a knife into my back. I thought moving to historic Savannah would let me relax a little. I forgot you were good with a knife."

"Think what you want as long as you are nowhere near this city tonight."

"No can do. I'm not going anywhere."

"Moran is coming for you. And Christina."

A chill ran up Marcus's spine. "She's safe. I made sure of it."

"If you say so. Personally, I wouldn't want to take such a risk. You should let me handle this."

"And let you frame me? No way."

Lucius's jaw ticked as he stared him down. "Have it your way, but when the dust settles, I can't promise that you won't have blood on your hands. Or your own spilled out. If you own a gun, you might want to have it by your side and loaded up. Everything goes down tonight."

Marcus leaned over to his right side to open his bottom drawer. His gun waited there. He took his eyes off the doorway for one second, but that was all his brother needed to disappear again.

"Now what?" Marcus shouted. "Are there going to be two of us running around this city tonight?"

Somewhere off in the building, Lucius responded in a deep voice. "You better pray that come morning there will still be two of us alive."

The slightest click of a door told Marcus he was alone again. Careless of his brother to let him hear him leave? Probably not. Lucius wanted him to know he was now alone in whatever came his way.

Whatever that was would be happening tonight.

But how was Marcus to fight against a masked enemy? The irony that his brother was now unmasked didn't go unnoticed.

What was he up to?

There was only one way to find out.

Marcus stood and walked to his closet. He removed his gray suit coat, opting for a black sport coat and black pants. He fought his battles in the courtroom but wasn't new to the streets. If that's where he had to return, then so be it.

"I CANNOT BELIEVE you never told me about Marcus," Mel said, laying on the opposite end of the sofa. Chris sat cross-legged on the other end with a cup of tea in her hands.

"There wasn't much to tell. Or at least I thought there wasn't. As far as I was concerned, he was out of my life for good."

"But he looked for you." Mel sat up.

"So he says."

"Why would Marcus lie? Now, after becoming a Christian and choosing the straight and narrow life. I say give him another chance."

Chris put her teacup down on the side table. "You haven't even met him. Why would you defend him like this?"

"Because you love him."

Chris sputtered. "I do not. That's absurd."

"Is it? Chris, I have rarely seen you date anyone."

"My life was complicated. I couldn't bring someone into it. Besides, opening Club Creare meant more to me. Not as much as it meant to you, but it kept me busy."

Mel smiled and closed her eyes. "I miss working at the club." Her eyes widened. "But I love my life with Jeremy and could never go back. Rafe is going to blow his top when he hears you aren't coming back either."

"Who said I wasn't going back?" Chris scooted away, feeling affronted by her friend's accusation.

Mel scooted closer, studying Chris intently. "Hear me out. You know I love you, and it's because I love you that I want you to follow your heart."

"Following my heart already proved to be a bad choice. I know you mean well, and going home for you worked out amazingly well, but it won't for me. Savannah can't be my home anymore. And it's the only home that Marcus knows. I could never take him out of it."

"Don't you hear yourself?" Mel grabbed her hands. "I could shake you right now. Stop trying to take care of everyone else and take care of yourself for once. You matter too. You don't have to live a life of sacrifice. You were meant for more."

Mel leaned toward the back of the sofa as Chris pondered her words. "You make it sound so easy."

She turned her head toward Chris. "When I almost died because of my stubbornness and addiction you were honest with me. No matter how much it hurt to hear you say I had a problem, you were right. Well, Chris, you have a problem too. You're not living your life."

"I just said I love working at the club."

"But it's not your dream. It was mine. It was always mine, and I had to let it go so I could live again. What's your dream?"

Chris didn't have to think long or hard.

Mel tugged on her hand. "Go ahead, say it. We both know the answer."

Tears filled Chris's eyes. "To...dance." She sniffed and swiped at her eyes with the palm of her hand. "Ballet is all I ever wanted to do. I may not have been good enough to dance the styles for Broadway, but Freddie gave me every opportunity to dance ballet here, even if it was probably because Vincent Moran is my father. Still, aside from leaving Marcus, leaving the theater hurt almost as much."

"I'm glad to hear you admit that leaving Marcus did hurt you."

"Of course, it did. I loved him, even if it wasn't reciprocal. I understand why he had to use me to take down my father. I really understand now. I don't hold it against him anymore."

The soft rap on the back door pulled their attention toward the kitchen.

Chris stretched her legs and stood. "That will be Marcus. Care to meet him?"

Mel clapped her hands giddily. "I wouldn't miss this for the world. In fact, I'll beat you to the door."

Mel raced past Chris, but she caught up with her in the doorway. The two squeezed through, giggling the rest of the way to the back door.

The overhead light glowed a soft yellow and revealed Marcus still in his suit but standing off to the side in the shadows.

Chris opened the door and said, "Come in. I want to introduce you to Mel."

"I really don't have time to meet him right now. It's late." Marcus's words were low almost hushed.

"No. My friend Melody. What is wrong with you? You know who Mel is. I've talked about her many times."

"If you say so. Look, it's late. I'd like you to come back with me where I can keep an eye on you tonight."

Something was wrong. "You don't think I'm safe here? What about everyone else? Jeremy, Sam, Gloria, they're already in bed. Should I wake them up?"

"No. They're fine. It's you I'm worried about." Marcus looked out into the darkness, only raising the hair on the back of her neck more. "We need to go."

"Okay. Let me just say goodbye." Chris reluctantly turned around and opened her arms to Mel. "Take good care of Sam. I'll be there as soon as I can."

Mel studied Marcus's profile in the shadows. She chewed on her lower lip in consternation. Turning away from the door, she whispered, "You like him? He doesn't seem very nice."

Chris had to agree there was something wrong with his behavior. But he had his reasons, and they were valid. "He's going through a rough time right now. Perhaps, you'll have a second chance for a better first impression."

"I'll take your word for it, but I think I might have been wrong in my advice to you. This one I think you should run from again."

Chris pulled Mel in for a hug. "As I said, it's not an easy choice. I'll see you soon."

Chris opened the door wide and stepped out into the night. Marcus was already down the steps out of the light, and she ran up beside him.

"Where are we going?" she asked.

Marcus gave no response but continued walking down the street.

"Where's your car?"

Again, no answer.

"Why aren't you talking? What happened? And why were you so mean to Mel?"

"So many questions," he mumbled. "How does he handle this?"

"How does who handle what? Marcus, you're confusing me. Can we just stop walking and discuss the plan?"

He picked up his pace and walked faster. Chris did her best to keep up and soon found herself in a full run but had no idea where she was running to.

Then the view of the river, sparkling under the lights alerted her to their direction. Marcus stopped and scanned the area. Chris followed his gaze to see what he was looking at but could barely make out anything in the dark. All the restaurants were closed for the night, and the river drifted by silently and peacefully.

Nothing seemed out of the ordinary.

Then a tall figure stepped out from the tree with the outline of a gun by his side. In the next second, Marcus grabbed Chris by the neck and jammed what could only be a gun to the side of her head.

"Drop it, old man or she's dead."

"Let my daughter go." The unmistakable sound of her father's voice carried along the breeze.

But all Chris could focus on was the gun jammed at her temple and his chokehold blocking the air from her lungs. She quickly realized she had fallen for his lies again. "Marcus! What are you doing?" How wrong she had been about him. The moment she let her guard down, he only proved that he was using her to get to her father again. "Why are you doing this?"

"Shut it. I've had enough of your questions. Ask one more and I'll shoot you anyway."

Chris had no choice but to give in and give up.

CHAPTER 13

MARCUS TAPPED on the glass window to Gloria's back kitchen door. All the lights inside were off, and he figured Chris had gone to bed for the night. He should just leave her be, but what if danger came knocking during the night? She was safer with him, no matter what.

He tapped again just as a light turned on in the kitchen. A man in plaid shorts and a T-shirt squinted his way.

"Can I help you?" The man held a gun in his hand, and instant panic surged in Marcus.

"Let me in," he demanded.

"Not until you tell me who you are," the strange man said. Was he one of Vincent's henchmen?

"Marcus. Who are you?"

185

"Jeremy." The man unlocked the door and step back. "What are you doing back? And where's Chris?"

Marcus looked toward the stairs. "She'd better be here. I told her to stay and wait for me."

"Jeremy?" A short woman with curly brown hair stepped off the stairs. "What's going on?"

"Marcus says he came to get Chris. I thought she left."

The woman rushed into the kitchen. "You're not Marcus I mean maybe you look like him, but you're wearing different clothes."

"What? No, no, no…are you telling me Chris went with a man looking like me but wearing a suit?"

"Yes, that's exactly what I'm saying. Are you telling me you're Marcus?"

"I am Marcus Cartwright. The man that Chris went with is my twin, Lucius."

"Oh, thank God," the woman said.

"No, there's nothing to thank God about here. Lucius means trouble. I need to know where he took her."

"Took her? Is Chris in danger?"

"Very much so. Where did they go?"

The woman grabbed at her head. "I could only

see them for a little while. But they went to the left. They were walking fast and then disappeared into the dark. I lost them after that. I figured she knew what she was doing by going with him, even though I didn't really like it very much. I was surprised she loved someone like that. He was kind of mean."

"That's being nice about it. And just so you know, I love her too." Marcus turned around to head back out the door.

Jeremy called after him, "Let me go with you."

"No. Stay with the women and keep that gun by your side the whole time. Got it? Don't let anyone in."

"You don't have to tell me twice. We'll be praying you find Chris in time."

"Thank you. Yes, God, keep her safe." Marcus took off in a run and could only hope he was heading in the right direction. He didn't know why Lucius would kidnap Chris by pretending to be him, but it couldn't be good. Impersonating him was one thing, but tricking Chris to go with him crossed the line.

Marcus felt for his gun in the holster at his side. If he had to use it on his brother tonight, he would. He put his hand on the butt and pulled it out. The

Glock fit snugly in his hand as he kept it at the ready.

He ran through the grid of streets, hoping he wasn't running in the wrong direction. Every alley he passed, he scanned, and every street he looked up and down for any sign of movement. Every couple strolling around that he passed, he brought his gun to his side and moved closer to identify them.

Savannah had never felt so large and over-whelming.

He stopped in one of the squares just as a gunshot echoed through the night.

"The river," he said aloud and took off in a run again. Four streets over, three streets down, and two more gunshots through the night.

By now, dogs were barking and lights were turning on, but Marcus pushed himself past his limits, denying what he would find when he reached the waterfront.

Suddenly, a voice in the shadows spoke. "Boss says we need to stay out here on the outskirts. Something's going down."

Marcus stumbled to a halt while his chest heaved from exertion. He quickly pushed up against a building and out of the streetlights. "What?" He didn't know who this man was and squinted through the dark to find where he was hiding. "Identify yourself."

"It's me Freddie. What is wrong with you, Lucius?"

Lucius?

Right, Lucius is pretending to be me, he thought to himself. *Freddie thinks I'm Lucius.*

"Slow night at the theater?" Marcus tried to act nonchalant.

"No show tonight. I'm on street duty."

It was no wonder Moran was always three steps ahead of everyone else and could never be caught in his crimes. The man had men lurking in shadows all over the city. "Who's shooting? What's going down?"

"I'm surprised you don't know, being Moran's hidden Ace in the Hole. The boss is getting his daughter back tonight. Man, I wish Christina stayed away. I believed she was free. But I guess we both know freedom is a façade. Moran will always win in the end."

Hidden Ace in the Hole? Marcus did his best not to growl in anger at his brother. Lucius was his mole. Marcus glanced toward the riverfront, needing to be there but also not wanting to alert Freddie to his true identity.

"How long have you worked for Moran?" *Is there anyone in this city who doesn't?*

Freddie grunted. "It must be going on thirty years now, you?"

Marcus didn't have an answer to that question. Had Lucius been involved with Moran's dealings their whole life? Even while they lived on the west side? Even while Lucius was in the military?

"Not sure," Marcus answered truthfully.

Freddie laughed. "I understand. It's not like we're working toward a pension. We're just trying to pay our bills. Moran keeps you in the shadows. You must be pretty important to be the man with no face."

Marcus hated hearing about his brother's honored placement in Moran's business. "Do you know why I took the job?" He couldn't help asking.

Freddie grunted again. "Eh, we don't usually ask. We all have our reasons, but I did hear you were a tribute."

A tribute? As in Lucius took someone's place? Whose?

Two more gunshots blasted to the night, jerking Marcus back against the wall. They sounded close.

"I'm going in," he said.

Freddie stepped out of the shadows with his hands up to block him. "Directions were to stand guard and watch for Marcus and apprehend him. Once we have your brother, Toby will go and get Christina. We know where Marcus is hiding her."

Marcus pressed harder against the wall. He couldn't let Freddie see him directly. He would realize he was talking to the real Marcus. In the shadows, he thought through Freddie's statement. The man didn't know that Lucius already had Christina. But why didn't he know? And why had his brother veered from the plan and taken her early but not told Moran's team? Marcus needed to get down to the river ASAP. That's all he did know.

There was only one way to get by Freddie without raising any flags.

"There's been a change of plans. I guess you hadn't heard. Marcus took Christina out of the house. That shooting you're hearing is the boss needing our help. I'm going in."

Freddie huffed and turned toward the river. "Why am I always the last to know?"

Before the man took off, Marcus said, "Freddie, I think you should go home. I got this. Don't you have a wife?"

"Yes, and I love her dearly. Are you sure about this? Moran gave me directions to wait here."

Marcus wanted to tell him that his days of being

a henchman were coming to an end, but could he really promise such a thing?

"That was before Lu—*Marcus* got word of the plan. Looks like he rushed things and caught Moran by surprise. And yes, go home. This is what I'm for. The man in the shadows. The Ace in the Hole. The man for the surprises. I'm not married. I have no connections to anyone. If I die, who will miss me?"

Marcus realized instantly what his brother had done tonight.

The tribute…*for him*. It was why Moran left him alone. First Reggie, and then Lucius stood in his place.

As Freddie turned to head home, Marcus said, "Four years. I've been working for Moran for four years…to keep him away from my brother."

Freddie put up his hands. "As I said, we all have our reasons. Be safe out there."

Marcus waited for the sounds of his footsteps to disappear and then took off in a run. He had no idea how many men were waiting and how many had jumped in to help. Judging by the five gunshots he heard, there could be a couple.

He could only hope those bullets had not found their mark.

And he still may never forgive his brother for

tricking Chris into going with him. He could only hope he had gotten her to safety before the bullets started flying.

Except, as he reached the riverfront, he immediately saw that wasn't the case.

The site of Lucius holding Chris in a chokehold with the gun to her head nearly brought him to his knees.

Another blast went off, sparking a flash from the trees by the river. The shooter was hidden, and their bullet went up into the night sky. Marcus was glad he wasn't shooting at Chris, but he hated seeing his brother hold her in such a paralyzing position.

"Let her go!" Marcus shouted at the top of his lungs. His feet were practically lifting in the air as he raced into the fray.

"No!" his brother shouted back, but it didn't sound like an order. It sounded desperate. Marcus didn't think he had ever heard Lucius sound so frantic. "Go home, brother. This has nothing to do with you."

A cackle from the trees echoed and rumbled into a burst of deep laughter. "Actually, Marcus, this has everything to do with him. Get my daughter, Lucius, and bring her to me. And while you're at it, put a bullet in your brother's head. He killed my son, and now he will die for it."

The shooter was Vincent Moran….and he thought Marcus was Lucius, his Ace in the Hole, come to do his dirty work.

Marcus stood frozen on what his next move would be. He felt as though he was in the courtroom standing between the DA and the jury. He had one chance to end Moran's authority and persuade Lucius to go along with him.

"I know what you did," Marcus said to his brother. "But you don't have to take care of me anymore. You can walk away right now. Let Christina go and let me finish this."

Lucius tightened his hold on Christina causing her to choke a little. He kept the gun pressed to her temple. "You don't know what you're asking for. You will never be free again. There is no finishing it if he gets what he wants tonight."

"Bring me my daughter, *now*," Moran demanded in a lethal tone. "Kill him!"

Marcus moved slowly toward his brother. "You're hurting her. Just let her go. I know you don't want to hurt her. It's part of the act."

Lucius sent him a heated glare. "You're ruining everything," he spoke through gritted teeth.

"No, I'm bringing the truth to light. No more living in the shadows. No more paying tribute to protect me. We're not some kids on the street anymore. We made it out alive, and I am not going to let either of us die tonight."

Moran stepped from the trees. His gun was in his hand at the ready. "You were given directions. Disobey my orders, and I will shoot you right now."

"I'm not killing my brother," Marcus said, turning his head a bit, but keeping Lucius in his view as well. "Take her away, Lucius. This is my fight. It has always been my fight."

Moran lifted his gun and aimed it at him. "Then you have ceased to be valuable to me. Goodbye, Lucius…no, *Marcus*." Moran chuckled with a growing grin as he realized Marcus had given the secret of identities away when he called his brother his real name. "A little game of switching places. How cute. You're right, Marcus, this is our fight. But first." Moran turned his gun quickly on Lucius and shot his gun instantly with no warning.

Lucius flew back, releasing his hold on Chris as he fell back to the ground.

"No!" Marcus ran toward Lucius and Chris. She also fell to the ground in a struggling and gasping heap.

In the next second, three more gunshots blasted through the air. The dirt and cobblestones around Marcus sprayed up where the bullets hit and ricocheted. Marcus scrambled toward Chris, expecting to be hit at any moment. Vincent was out for blood but reaching her was all Marcus cared about. Even if he died beside her. He lifted his own gun as he rolled to Chris and faced Moran. The man took aim and smiled.

"Your hand is shaking, Marcus. You don't have the guts to pull that trigger. Too bad." Moran pulled his and a gun blast louder than any other that night wrenched through the air. Marcus turned his face and waited for the final blow. But then the gunshots stopped, and all went still.

CHRIS GRABBED at her neck and heaved for air while Marcus lay motionless beside her. Her father's shot had found its mark right in his chest. As Lucius reached for Chris, she pushed him away and got on her knees to try and breathe. Air still wouldn't go in.

"Try to breathe slowly," Lucius said, thankfully keeping his distance. Still, she waved him away.

"It's me. It's me Marcus. I promise you. I had

nothing to do with this. I didn't use you. I know that's what you're thinking. I love you, Chris. Please, believe me."

Chris sat back, feeling her eyes widen in shock. Then she glanced to the left and couldn't breathe for a whole different reason.

"He's...dead," she said in a raspy voice, looking across the cobblestones toward Moran.

Marcus turned away from her to see her father sprawled in an unnatural position. His eyes were wide and still. His mouth gaped with his last breath never taken.

"But who shot him?" Marcus asked aloud, looking at the gun in his own hand. "Lucius never had a chance to take a shot, and I didn't pull the trigger."

Chris looked between Lucius and the man lying next to her. The man she thought was Marcus. Realization settled within her. "He pretended to be you?"

"Yes," Marcus said. He moved a little closer to her, but she was unsure if she was ready to receive him just yet, and her hands went up to hold him off. "I would never do that to you. He thought he was helping me."

"I was." Lucius suddenly groaned beside her. *The real Lucius.* "I had it all worked out." Lucius elbowed his way up with a grunt. He tore the dress shirt away, popping buttons to reveal his bulletproof vest beneath the suit disguise. "Come out, Diane. It's over."

"Diane?" Chris pushed herself to her feet as Diane Brodsky stepped from behind a trashcan.

Diane held a gun in her hand but not pointed at anyone. It was the evidence that she had been the one to take down Vincent Moran.

"He killed Reggie," she explained with pleading eyes directed at Chris. "When he shot Marcus, I shot him. He would have killed Marcus too. I know what it feels like to lose the man you love. I had no choice but to shoot him. I hope you understand."

"My brother didn't kill Reggie?" Chris asked, taking a step closer to Diane.

She shook her head. "I saw Vincent do it. I followed Reggie to the apartment construction site because I knew he was going to make another deal that would keep us under Vincent's thumb forever. I wanted to stop him."

Diane's lips trembled as she pressed back the tears. "But then, Reggie told Vincent that he had what he needed to put him away. Reggie told him about the misuse of funds and the poor construction. That Vincent was pocketing the allocated money instead. Reggie told him that he would never be under his thumb again. And as my husband turned to leave, Vincent killed him instantly by hitting him over the head with a glass bottle. It shattered in pieces as my husband bled out. I stayed hidden so Vincent didn't know I was there. I watched him cut a beam and run out. I think he meant for the place to cave in on Reggie. I tried to lift Reggie but couldn't. I went to find Lucius, but when we returned the body was gone. After, I tried to keep the bottle pieces in hopes it could be used to convict his murderer. But I didn't know which police I could trust. You found one of the pieces when you were at my house. I must have dropped it when I arrived home that night. I threw it away so your prints wouldn't be found on it."

"It still had blood on it." Chris remembered holding the shard.

"My Reggie's." Tears spilled down Diane's cheeks.

Chris reached Diane and took her into her arms. "I'm so sorry. How scary for you that you thought you had to flee your home in order to be safe. That you couldn't go to the police. That's not right or just."

Diane stared at Chris and touched her face. "I knew you were nothing like him. When you came to see me, I told you what evidence Reggie was gathering on your father, but you said you didn't think he was guilty. I was afraid you would tell him what I said, and I got scared and left town immediately. I was afraid Vincent would come for me next. I feared he might have seen me at the apartment site that night. But then Lucius found me and brought me back to end this forever. I didn't mean to kill him. Lucius's plan was just to get him to confess to murdering Reggie. I was here to tell Vincent what I saw him do. We were going to pretend to bargain you for the confession. You're all he wanted. I guess he cared about you in a weird and twisted way."

Chris shook her head. "He cared about control. I was the last Moran he could control."

"Still, I'm sorry we had to use you."

Chris turned to face Lucius, now on his feet. She glanced at Marcus as well. "Am I the only one who didn't know about this plan? A little notice would have been nice. My heart still hasn't slowed down." She touched her neck. "I can feel my neck already bruising."

Marcus walked to her. "I didn't know, honey. I promise."

Lucius pulled the bulletproof vest away from his chest so he could rub the spot the bullet had hit right over his heart. "That man was a good shot. I'll give him that. Anyway, I couldn't tell either of you. It was too risky." He waved a hand at Marcus. "You're too much into your head and *the law* to go along with us." He pointed at Chris. "And you, you're a Moran. Why would I tell you?"

Chris huffed and stood tall to face him. "I am a DePalo."

"You may want to reconsider that," Lucius said with a smirk and a chuckle. "You're now a very wealthy woman. Moran never changed his will because he always planned to bring you back, whether you liked it or not. In fact, Silas only went to kill you when he went to New York City, so he could be sure he was the last Moran. He was so jealous of you. For twelve years, all he heard from his father was how you were the better child. You would be dead if you had been at home that night. But now, you are the last Moran, take it or leave it."

Tears of frustration filled her eyes, and she shook her head in denial. "I want nothing to do with his money."

Lucius walked to Diane and took the gun, pocketing it in the suit coat. "No one said you had to keep it. Let's go, Diane. We were never here. I suggest the two of you hightail it out of here too."

Marcus looked around. "Where are the police? And the rest of Moran's goons?"

Lucius had his arm wrapped around Diane and as he passed Marcus, he flashed him a grin. "The police had the night off. And the goons are all probably going home to their families. No boss? No orders to follow. They're free tonight, too. All you have to know is it's over. I'll call the body in."

Marcus stood stunned, shaking his head as he watched his brother disappear into the shadows again. "Who do you work for?" Marcus asked for the third time that night, even knowing he would never get a straight answer.

Suddenly, Chris laughed and covered her lips. He reached for her, and she ran right into his arms.

"It's over," she said against his neck. "I can't believe it's over. I'm finally free."

Marcus glanced Moran's way, and she followed his focus. The man was really dead. Marcus said, "He's not coming back from this one. Let's go."

Marcus wrapped his arm around her and pulled her close. She rested her head on his shoulder as they walked in silence, each processing the night's events.

"I'm so glad you're with me," she said, reaching for his hand. "It seems fitting that we would end this together, after, well, after he stood between us for so long."

Marcus leaned over and kissed her forehead. "I meant what I said. I love you, Chris DePalo. I always have."

Chris smiled against him. "You can call me Christina Moran if you want to. I'm going to change the meaning of the name if it's the last thing I ever do."

Marcus chuckled. "I always knew you were one strong woman, and I know you will do it. You will take Savannah by storm."

"I'm going to start with the kids in the neighborhood. Right after I pay your taxes," she giggled. "I'm going to need an attorney on retainer, and I want nothing but the best. Brodsky and Cartwright, Attorneys at Law. I hear they always win."

Marcus stopped and pulled her into his arms. "I sure feel like a winner tonight." He moved in and claimed her lips, not that she planned to ever withhold them from him again.

Chris lifted her face for only a moment. "I've always loved you too. I wish I had known you looked for me. But I won't hide from you anymore."

Marcus brushed her lips with his thumb and moved his hand to the side of her face. "Then you better not get used to the Moran name, sweetheart. Christina Cartwright does have a nice ring to it too, don't you think?"

Chris laughed as tears pricked her eyes again. "Don't tease me unless you mean it, Marcus Cartwright."

"I have never been more serious, Chris. You are it for me. You always were. You're stuck with me, and if I must debate this further, you should know I have gone eight hours straight in the courtroom without breaking a sweat. And I always make my point."

Chris looked to the skies. "I wish my mother was here to see this. She would have loved you nearly as much as I do." Chris wrapped her arms around him, never wanting to let him go again.

Rejoicing that she didn't have to.

"This feels better than any case I have ever won," he whispered against her ear. "You know why?"

She shook her head and swiped at her tears. "Why?"

"Because we let God have His vengeance and didn't take it into our own hands. He's going to bless us because of this, Chris. He avenged us all tonight, including your mother."

Chris searched the starry sky and smiled. "It's over, Mom." Looking back at Marcus, she took his hand. "Jeremy must be having a fit right now. We should get back and let them know everyone is safe."

As they made their way back to Gloria's, they noticed the lights were all on downstairs, and Chris ran up the steps to be enveloped in a hug by Mel once again.

"Are you okay?" She demanded to know.

Chris nodded and glanced at Jeremy who was fully clothed with his gun in his hand. "He's dead. My father is dead."

Jeremy put the gun away and grabbed a chair at the table. "You girls really know how to age a man," he said. "Are there any other bad guys in your past that I should know about?"

Chris laughed with Mel because he wasn't wrong. "Did we take another ten years off your life, Jeremy?"

"At least. I should've gone with you. I hated sitting here, waiting for trouble to come knocking." He looked at Marcus, "So are you the real Marcus this time?"

Marcus held out his hand to Jeremy. "Yes, I apologize for my brother. He has a flair for the dramatic. You never really know what he's going to be dressed up as."

"Sounds like an interesting fellow."

Mel interrupted, "Well, I'm so glad that you're the real Marcus. Because your brother is not very nice. I was all set to kidnap Chris myself. Speaking of which, would you come back with us tomorrow?"

Chris glanced at Marcus and put her hand out. As soon as he touched her and stepped close, she said, "Actually, I'm staying in the Savannah. Permanently. I have a lot of work I can do here. I'm needed here."

Marcus smiled at her. "By me. I need her. Please don't take her away."

Jeremy laughed, resting an arm on the table. "Oh man, I know exactly how you feel. I'm glad to see you embrace it. So, when's the wedding?"

Chris sputtered. "We haven't gotten that far. We just know we never want to be separated again."

Mel glanced at her husband and nodded. "I understand." She took a deep breath and let out a long sigh. "However, Rafe Sinclair is running the restaurant all by himself now. I don't know if he is going to be as understanding. We need to approach this with a strategic plan, or he will go ballistic."

Chris thought of Rafe's temper, and how he went 0 to 60 in 2.3 seconds. Rafe's good food wasn't the only thing hot in the kitchen. He had a temper to match.

"I hadn't thought about Rafe," Chris said, chewing on her bottom lip. She looked at her future husband with a desperate plea for help.

Marcus flashed her his beautiful smile. "Don't worry, I've been known to take care of my clients very well. I have reason to believe that a well-drawn-up agreement keeps all parties satisfied at the table. And if the man still thinks he's going to keep you, the gloves will come off and I will fight him to the death."

Chris laughed and mock-punched Marcus in the gut. "Rafe will have no idea who he's up against. It would be in his best interest to go along with the agreement, I think."

"I concur. And for the record, October in Savannah is the best time for a wedding. So what do you say, do we have a deal?"

Chris bit her lip and looked at Mel. "Can you get back here that soon?"

"I wouldn't miss it for the world. Say yes to him, or I will say yes for you." Mel beamed a bright smile, full of support and love. Mel may think that Chris saved her life, but Chris knew the rescue was mutual.

Chris faced her future husband, the love of her

life. "I say October sounds perfect to become your wife, Marcus. Yes, I will marry you."

Marcus leaned in to kiss her, but a sound on the stairs pulled all their attention. Then Gloria and Sam stepped into the kitchen. They rubbed their eyes from sleep. Sam asked, "What's going on? Why is everyone up in the middle of the night? Is there a problem?"

Chris looked nervously at Marcus, and Marcus looked at Jeremy for help while Mel burst out at the top of her lungs, "They're getting married!"

A NOTE FROM KATY

Dear Reader,

Thank you for joining me in Savannah, Georgia for Chris and Marcus's journey back to each other. Even in the sweltering heat of summer, love can be found. If you would like to read Mel and Jeremy's journey, you can check out *Real Virtue* wherever books are sold. Ebooks, Print and audio are also available on my website, KatyLeeBooks.com.

Happy Reading!
Katy Lee

FREE SHORT STORY!

Sign up for more book updates and my monthly "Novel Ideas" Newsletter that goes out every full moon and receive a **FREE** short story ebook https://dl.bookfunnel.com/4p9kuzeuet

Table for One. Left at the altar may just be the best thing that's ever happened to her.

Becca Shane has a cruise to catch, even if she's now boarding her honeymoon solo.

Patrick Joyce has a daughter to raise after his wife turned her back on him when he needed her the most.

Neither believe in love, but can they believe in each other?

Table for One is the prequel to the up-and-coming Royal Bay Billionaire Beach Club, where money can lead to love...or murder...or both.

Happy Reading!
Katy

actual target, his plan for reconciliation turns to one of protection-whether she wants his help or not. What he wants are answers, especially about this online game she plays. Is it a harmless *pastime,* as she says? Or is she using it to cover something up? As a faceless predator destroys the things that matter to her, Jeremy knows he's running out of time before she loses the one thing that matters most-her real life.

Real Justice

Book Two in the Web of Lies series

A ransom note left in her apartment tells Christina Depalo that changing her name and hiding in the big city hadn't been enough to escape her dangerous family. The Morans have kidnapped her roommate, demanding Christina return to Georgia. But that will mean facing the cutthroat attorney Marcus Cartwright, a man she once loved but who only wanted to take down her family.

Marcus had started a coalition with his friend to crack down on organized crime in Savannah. But when his friend loses his life in a supposed accident, nothing will stop Marcus from seeking justice, not even the Moran's prodigal daughter who left town twelve years ago. Nobody will derail him this time.

But then Christina never was a nobody.

happened long ago—or more recently. Island sheriff Wesley Grant seems sure the murder didn't happen on *his* watch. But when Lydia uncovers the victim's identity, someone goes to great lengths to get Lydia off the island. Wes vows to protect her, but is the handsome lawman holding something back? To help catch a killer, she'll have to trust him—or become the next victim.

~

Sunken Treasure

Stepping Stones Island Series Book 3

DANGER ON THE HIGH SEAS

Shipwreck diver Gage Fontaine is used to modern-day pirates chasing after his boat and the buried treasure he salvages. But when he unknowingly leads a dangerous criminal to the waters off Stepping Stones Island, he puts a beautiful fisherwoman in grave danger. Rachelle Thibodaux has spent the past year hiding on her boat to avoid the town's censure for her father's crimes. But when she comes face-to-face with a gun-wielding pirate, she becomes a new kind of target. To save her own life, she'll have to work with Gage to find the treasure before the pirates do.

~

Permanent Vacancy

Stepping Stones Island Series Book 4

BUYER BEWARE

When Gretchen Bauer begins renovating an old Victorian
house to turn it into a bed-and-breakfast, she barely
escapes several dangerous "accidents" at her home. Colm
McCrae, host of the home improvement TV show helping
her renovate, refuses to believe these aren't on purpose.
Could this be a harmful ploy by his boss to boost ratings?
Yet with Colm's Irish brogue and handsome face,
Gretchen wonders whether he could be involved. But with
a whole town full of neighbors disgruntled about the inn
bringing strangers to their shores, Gretchen has a list of
more likely suspects. Now she must trust Colm if she
wants to keep her new business venture from turning into
a five-star death trap.

Silent Night Pursuit

Roads to Danger Series Book 1: Family secrets resurface

RACE AGAINST TIME

Lacey Phillips believes Captain Wade Spencer knows
something about her brother's mysterious death. So she
throws caution to the wind and tracks him down on

Christmas Eve looking for answers. Wade tries to turn her away—until bullets start to fly. He doesn't want to take the stubborn beauty on his life-or-death mission to find out the truth about how Wade's past may have cost her brother his life. But with killers lurking everywhere, he has to protect her—especially when she breaches the walls around his heart. Can Wade and his faithful service dog keep Lacey alive long enough to figure out who's targeting them?

Blindsided / Ransom Rescue

Roads to Danger Series Book 2: Family secrets resurface

UNDERCOVER RESCUE

When race-car track owner Veronica Spencer discovers stolen cars in a garage on her track, she knows she's been framed. But before Roni can do anything about it, the criminals kidnap her. Undercover FBI agent Ethan Gunn shouldn't break his cover to protect Roni, but he won't watch her die, either. Despite his FBI information that says she's involved in the crime ring, Ethan knows she's innocent. So he risks it all to help her break free. But now, with killers and the FBI on their trail, Ethan must find a way to keep her safe...and clear her name.

High Speed Holiday

Roads to Danger Series Book 3: Family secrets resurface

TANGLED PAST

After Ian Stone discovers he was kidnapped when he was a baby, he journeys to his "family's" hometown—and is shot at shortly after he arrives. Now he's convinced the Spencers don't want their long-lost brother, Luke, to return and claim his inheritance. But local chief of police Sylvie Laurent doesn't believe his siblings would try to kill him. And the stubborn woman is determined to protect him until she uncovers the truth. At first, Sylvie is skeptical of Ian's story…but he bears a strong resemblance to the Spencers. And they'll have to work together to stay ahead of the danger if they want to live to see him reunited with his family at Christmas.

~

Amish Country Undercover

Rogues Ridge Setting

Secrets, sabotage and small-town danger. *Someone wants an Amish woman dead.*

Taking the reins of her father's Amish horse-trading business, Grace Miller's prepared for backlash over breaking community norms—but not for sabotage. Now someone's willing to do anything it takes to make sure she fails, and it's undercover FBI agent Jack Kaufman's mission to stop them. But can Jack face his own Amish past long enough to shield Grace from a killer?

Amish Sanctuary

Rogues Ridge Setting

A woman on the run. A baby in danger. Can her Amish ex-fiancé save them?

To keep her patient's baby safe from a killer, counselor Naomi Kemp will do things she never thought possible, like return to her Amish hometown…and her ex-fiancé. Widower Sawyer Zook can offer Naomi and the baby protection and a place to hide. But Sawyer can't shield Naomi from what threatens her most: the traumatic past that drove her away years ago…

Framed in Amish Country: A Novella

Rogues Ridge Setting

Despite the disapproval of her Amish community, teacher Lizzie Fisher has fought for an independent life—even going so far as to tutor at the English school. Alex Wilson, a young English painter hired to paint the school, is used to being ridiculed because of his learning disabilities. He questions why the smart, pretty, Amish woman treats him differently. When Alex finds himself framed for a crime, he believes there is no hope for him, but Lizzie is sure her community will come to his aid. Except, their forbidden relationship may give Lizzie the independence she thought she always wanted.

~

Holiday Suspect Pursuit

Mysteries in New Mexico Series Book 1

Unraveling a murder mystery...could unlock his lost memories...

After a murderer strikes, former deputy Jett Butler and his search-and-rescue dog must work with the sole witness—FBI agent Nicole Harrington. But Nicole's the ex-fiancée he left behind after a car accident gave him amnesia years ago. And in a fight to survive the holidays, remembering his past might be just as dangerous as facing the killer on their heels...

~

Cavern Cover Up

Mysteries in New Mexico Series Book 2

A suspicion that her father's murder is linked to a smuggling ring sends private investigator Danika Lewis pursuing a lead all the way to Carlsbad Caverns National Park. Teaming up with ranger Tru Butler to search deep off-limits caves for the missing artifacts is the fastest way to uncover the truth. But there's danger in the dark and a killer on the loose who will do anything to keep secrets hidden.

~

Santa Fe Setup

Mysteries in New Mexico Series Book 3

Soon after artist Luci Butler learns someone's been hiding drugs *inside her paintings* she also discovers ruthless criminals are aiming to silence her. Only her brother's coworker, Bard Holland, is on her side. The pair must race to clear her name and track a murderer straight into the unforgiving mountains of New Mexico. Despite Bard's determined protection, Luci is being drawn dangerously close into a killer's merciless endgame.

~

Christmas K-9 Unit Heroes

Danger comes to Denver for the holidays in this Publisher's Weekly Bestseller.

The clock is ticking in Silent Night Explosion by Katy Lee
- but can Jodie Chen trust the newest K-9 officer on the
force, Victor Abrams, and his dog to find a bomb and keep
her alive…despite Victor's shadowed past? And with
veterinarian Sydney Jones being targeted, K-9 Officer
Gavin Walker and his furry partner must stand between
her and certain death in Lenora Worth's Hidden
Christmas Danger.

~

K-9 National Park Defenders

A #1 Publisher's Weekly Bestseller!

**Start making plans for a superb night, ushering in your
holidays with these two riveting novellas!**

A Christmas skiing retreat turns treacherous when Pacific
Northwest K-9 Unit Officer Veronica Eastwood's sister is
kidnapped in North Cascades National Park—and only
rival Officer Parker Walsh can help her in Katy
Lee's Yuletide Ransom. And in Sharee Stover's
explosive Holiday Rescue Countdown, K-9 officers Dylan
Jeong and Brandie Weller must race against the clock in
Olympic National Park when they face a Christmas
parade bomb threat…and a killer from Dylan's past.

~

ABOUT KATY LEE

1 Publishers Weekly Best-selling author Katy Lee has written over thirty-five novels, filled with romance, suspense, and inspiration. She lives in the rugged beauty of the Utah mountains where she is also a special education teacher at a school for international students. Katy has earned a Master's degree in Global Studies and Professional Writing and coaches people worldwide with their writing projects. She is also the Founder and CEO of her non-profit Story Haven Writers, Inc., providing healing through writing. Keep up with Katy and her latest novels at KatyLeeBooks.com.

Interact with Katy Lee at:
Website: http://www.katyleebooks.com/

www.ingramcontent.com/pod-product-compliance
Lightning Source LLC
Chambersburg PA
CBHW010738130726
47899CB00015B/3375